KA DWARA

DOORWAY TO BHULOKA

VISHESH

notionpress
.com

INDIA · SINGAPORE · MALAYSIA

Notion Press

Old No. 38, New No. 6
McNichols Road, Chetpet
Chennai - 600 031

First Published by Notion Press 2019
Copyright © Vishesh 2019
All Rights Reserved.

ISBN 978-1-64733-560-1

I dedicate this book to my parents

CONTENTS

ACKNOWLEDGEMENTS

First and foremost, I would like to thank God for His blessings which made me write from the first word to the last.

This book would not be possible without the support and encouragement from my wife, Sukanya even though it took up many of our evenings and weekends. Whenever I stopped writing and went blank, it was her push that got me back to writing.

I extend my thanks to my brother, Shreyas and my wife Sukanya who have been constantly reviewing and giving me feedback from the start for every few pages that I had written.

I would also like to thank my father, Vamadevappa who has published over 15 books on Educational Psychology and my mother, Sudha for being a constant support for every decision and step I take. They inspire my brother and me to always follow our dreams despite all the obstacles we may face to fulfill it.

My gratitude goes out to my colleagues and friends who read the book and gave me their feedback which helped shape this book.

I would like to thank my editor, Manjunath Narayan who has diligently curated the book by editing, rewriting and rephrasing my words to make it crisper.

I would like to thank Professor Balaji Rao and Jagadish Sir to give my initial draft a thorough read and provide me feedback to make corrections wherever necessary.

I would like to thank Hari Harsha of Checkmate Studio for bringing out an amazing trailer video on this book.

I would like to thank Sanket Borle, my dear friend and an amazing artist who captured my imagination through his sketch. You can follow him at borlesanket on Instagram.

I would like to thank all the authors who have inspired me to write this story.

I would like to thank many of the YouTubers like Jenna Moreci and Meg LaTtore who guide first timers on how to write a novel.

I also thank Notion Press for publishing this book and reaching it to you.

I would like to thank all my family members who have encouraged me to write and publish this book.

I would like to thank all the teachers from whom I have learned. Like the Sanskrit saying 'Aksharam kalisidatham guru'.

I finally like to shout out a big thanks to you, my reader! I hope you enjoy reading this book and with your support I would like to continue writing more books to keep you engrossed.

PREFACE

If you have chosen this book to read, I want you to know that I am also a big fan of mythology like you are. Its intriguing mysteries drew me to write something about ancient mysteries which I have read and also watched on YouTube.

I was drawn into the amazing world created by Amish Tripathi's Shiva Trilogy which dragged me to read more and more mythological stories. I was fascinated with the style of storytelling from Christopher C Doyle's, The Mahabharata Quest which led me to narrate the story in the manner in which you are going to read it.

I have learnt more about mythological stories from the perspective of Sadhguru Jaggi Vasudev through his videos which led me to do more and more research.

I was greatly inspired by the Kannada movie Rama Rama Re... I enjoyed it and learnt the way to contemporize the teachings in mythological tales.

PROLOGUE

17th Feb 3102 BC

Krishna stood on the banks of the Saraswati River looking at the moon. Balaram approached him slowly from behind with wet eyes "We have lost our entire lineage in this war. The city which you had built with great love is burned down to ashes. Aren't you feeling disheartened?"

Brother Balaram, am I not the one who told Arjuna-

maya tatam idam sarvam jagad avyakta-murtina
mat-sthani sarva-bhutani na chaham teshvavasthitah
na cha mat-sthani bhutani pashya me yogam aishwaram
bhuta-bhrin na cha bhuta-stho mamatma bhuta-bhavanah

– **Bhagavad Gita Chapter 9 - verse 5 and 4**

Translation

This entire cosmic manifestation is pervaded by Me in My unmanifest form. All living beings' dwell in Me, but I do not dwell in them.

And yet, the living beings do not abide in Me. Behold the mystery of My divine energy! Although I am the Creator and Sustainer of all living beings, I am not influenced by them or by material nature.

Everything in universe has a time and My time in this form has come. This price had to be paid to Gandhari for her curse to come true.

Whatever happened in this great war was to keep My promise to the Manavas that I would protect them from the Danavas whenever they pose a threat to Bhuloka.

Now the Danavas cannot come back easily as I have closed the dwara forever.

It is your responsibility O great Adishesha to keep this secret out of the Danavas' reach in the coming ages.

Balaram stood on his knees and said, "Thanks my lord for allowing me to serve You in this life" and left his body to emerge as Adishesha, a giant white serpent with several heads.

Krishna looked at the Ocean and joined His hands, bent His head and said, "O great king of oceans take this land from where I stand, once leased from you to build a marvelous city for My subjects. Time has come to return it to you."

An arrow bolted towards Krishna's toe from a hunter. Krishna smiled and left His body as it fell down like a cloth removed from His soul.

The Ocean reclaimed the lands that were leased to Krishna.

Dec 26th, 1998

Dr Vishwanath was sitting outside his room tightly gripping his coffee mug. His four-year-old son was sleeping inside the room.

It was the coldest of months. Chilling evening winds sung the tragic days of Vishwanath's life. He felt as if he were weighing a mountain over his chest filled with emotions. Winds accompanied by snow were trying to push him back to his room but he did not sense the cold outside. His heart was burning inside as if it was on fire.

Lieutenants Ponnappa and Veerprathap Singh returned to the army camp from their daily rounds to the nearby villages and checkpoints.

They heard that their friend Archeologist Dr Vishwanath who had taken a break from researching on Mt Kailash had returned from home with his four-year-old son, Vedaant. When they went near his room, they wondered why such a thin and tall fellow was standing out in such freezing cold without wearing suitable winter clothes. They had never seen Vishwanath like this. They had always seen him well dressed, neatly combed and wearing spectacles.

Ponnappa went from behind and saw Vishwanath gripping his coffee mug as if he was going to break it. Ponnappa put his arms across Vishwanath's shoulders and asked, "What happened to you my friend?"

Tears came cascading down Vishwanath's cheeks. He felt as if a huge mountain was moved off his chest. Veerprathap and Ponnappa took him inside and covered him in warm blankets.

After a while, he explained the situation to them — the chain of events which led him to take the decision to bring Vedaant here with him. Vishwanath's eyes were still filled with tears and his voice was trembling.

"I feel ashamed about the things I have done; how can I separate a mother from her son? What might she be facing because of my one single decision? It would have broken her to pieces and shattered her dreams. But I could not have dragged her into this dangerous place after witnessing the things we did." Dr Vishwanath regretted committing a dreadful mistake.

"It's okay Vishwanath, it happens. We all commit mistakes, it's part of life. You call her and make her understand that she is the most important person in your life. I know for sure, she will forgive you. You did the right thing by not bringing them here, the things we saw still gives me the chills in my dreams," Ponnappa tried to console Vishwanath.

Veerprathap Singh did not know what they were talking about. Ponnappa was one of the bravest men he ever knew, he was almost six feet tall, with a well-built physique, a muscular torso and for god's sake even he was scared. He was waiting for any one of them to explain what had happened, Ponnappa had also just arrived from his hometown.

"Will you now tell me what you guys are talking about?" Veerprathap could not control his increasing anxiety.

Sounds of some Jeeps approaching the army camp broke their conversation. "I will go check on them, you guys prepare your answers for me," said Veerprathap with a smile and went out to check.

As Veerprathap went outside to check on the Jeeps, he saw some masked men approaching. He asked the security sepoys at the gates to check on them. As the masked men approached closer, they pulled out their AK-47s and started firing at the sepoys.

Ponnappa heard the gunshots and asked Vishwanath to lock the doors and not to open them at any cost and went out.

Ponnappa saw masked men approaching from all sides; most of their sepoys had fallen dead in the firing. Now,

Veerprathap and his sepoys' bullets went piercing through the enemy's defence. The masked men's retaliation with bombs had set the army camp on fire and shattered it into pieces.

Ponnappa went inside the main office and took his INSAS rifle, a light machine gun and came out with all guns blazing at the enemies.

Veerprathap and his team got some help and they came out of the gates and threw grenades at the enemy Jeeps. Amidst the sounds of the blast, he did not hear someone approaching him from behind. As he turned around, bang! Someone hit him with a wooden log. Veerprathap's vision got blurred, he turned around to look, could not keep his balance and fell to the ground.

The masked men collected Veerprathap and team's guns and entered the camp. Meanwhile, Ponnappa was fighting alone shooting most of the masked men. Death was coming in the form of a blizzard from all sides for Ponnappa. A few bullets did not stop him. Blood was pumping through his veins; bullets from his gun were raining on masked men.

The masked men's bullets pierced Ponnappa's bullet proof vest and went through his chest and torso, he fell and stood on his knees. Someone gave him a brutal hit on the back of his head with an iron rod. Blood spluttered out of his head. Death was daemonic that day.

Vishwanath's room door opened with a bang! Vedaant was asleep because of the drugs he had taken for fever. After a few blows, the door gave away. A few masked men entered and captured Vishwanath and as they looked at Vedaant, he requested them, "Please leave him alone, he is just a kid."

One of the masked men said, "Take the kid, he will be useful for us to get answers from this archaeologist."

Vedaant was in deep sleep under his warm blanket as if he were sleeping comfortably in his mother's lap with a gentle and innocent smile on his face.

One of the masked men wrapped Vedaant in the blanket and carried him over his shoulders.

They kidnapped both and took them in their Jeep and drove towards Mt Kailash.

After a while, Veerprathap regained consciousness and saw that the army camp had turned into a graveyard.

He looked around and saw a pool of blood with several dead bodies lying around. He tried to find his friends, Ponnappa and Vishwanath by turning each of the bodies.

Ponnappa was lying in a pool of blood surrounded by dozens of dead bodies of the masked men. The scene sang the heroics of Ponnappa. Veerprathap stood stunned by looking at the scene, his pain at the loss of his friend was too much but he stood there in attention and saluted him. The tale of his valor would inspire thousands of soldiers.

He went on to search for Vishwanath. He swung open the door to Vishwanath's room to find no one. He looked everywhere, Dr Vishwanath and Vedaant were nowhere to be found.

Chapter 1

TRIP TO MOUNT KAILASH

20 years later, Bangalore

Vivaant, the son of a single mother who had grown up in Bangalore was a sports enthusiast and a champion at college. Being an athlete, he had a good physique. He was a regular visitor to the gym and was over six feet tall with well-developed muscles and abs.

He had finally finished his last semester exams. He knew he would get a decent score; he never worried about marks, as he somehow always cleared his exams in first class, even when he spent only a night before the exam for serious study with his friends.

Soon after finishing college, he was gearing up for the most awaited trip of his lifetime to the Himalayas which he had won after becoming the sports champion of the college.

Another student who had won the trip to the Himalayas was the champion in the girls' category – Sukheshni, known as one of the beautiful and intelligent girls at college. She used to get proposals every now and then. She always friend-zoned them. She was clear in her intentions to have all these relationships once she was out of college and started her career.

The Sports Fest of this academic year was sponsored by Dhithi Sports Academy who had announced the First Prize in both boys' and girls' categories — "An unforgettable trip to Mt Kailash."

Vivaant didn't like her much and neither did she like him. Sukheshni envied him for becoming the college champion as he would win more medals in group events like cricket in which girls could not participate and finally Vivaant would become the sports champion by winning a few more medals. On the flip side, Vivaant hated her as the professors would quote her as an example asking him to be excellent like her at both sports and studies.

Both had finished college. Sukheshni went on a full-fledged shopping spree and purchased everything required for trekking in the Himalayas while Vivaant didn't have that privilege of buying new things. He borrowed the necessary things from his friends and packed some stuff from his yearly treks to Kumara Parvatha.

Vivaant was a responsible child from his childhood as he had seen his mother struggle to fulfill the family needs after being deserted by his father. He tried to help his mother as much as he could. They were the best of friends and their love and care towards each other had no bounds.

Suvidha, Vivaant's mother was very much worried to be without her son for almost a month. She had to be alone in Bangalore but didn't want to curb Vivaant's excitement of his trek to the Himalayas and for the first time, he was going on an airplane.

Vivaant was also concerned about his mother, "Mom if you need anything when I am away, please let me know. I will ask one of my friends to attend to it," Vivaant expressed his concern.

Vivaant always wore a chain which had a pendant made of bluestone in pencil or sword shape. Suvidha looked at the silver chain that Vivaant wore and said, "This was given by your father when he met me for the last time, I don't know where he is but please don't lose it, and this is the only thing that is left to remember him."

"I don't want it; I don't even want to remember the person who deserted you. I don't know, why you even think of him to hurt yourself. He has given us nothing but pain," Vivaant reprimanded her in an angry tone.

Suvidha felt sad. Vivaant cheered her up, "Mom, tell me what you need. I will bring whatever you ask."

"I want your safe return with a big smile," said Suvidha. Their conversation was stopped by Vivaant's friends barging into the room and asking Suvidha to serve them tasty snacks. Suvidha was an excellent cook. His friends were waiting in a queue to get crispy butter dosas on their plates. The coconut-coriander chutney and boiled potatoes with a tadka of onion and chilli made it a perfect combination with butter dosas.

Vivaant's friends stayed back helping him to pack for the trip and teasing that he would enjoy the company of the most beautiful girl in college. One of his friends showed the pictures of them trekking at Kumara Parvata, Ballarayana Durga fort and the time when they tried to explore the unexplored scenic beauty of South Goa. They hadn't noticed the time, the clock struck 3 a.m. They called for an Uber cab and Vivaant woke up his mother.

Suvidha accompanied Vivaant and his friends in the cab to the airport. His friends were guiding him as it was his first flight.

"Vivaant call me every day," Suvidha said as she was worried about him.

"Don't worry aunty, he is going to be with the most beautiful girl from our college, he won't even remember you." One of his friends taunted him.

Vivaant hit his head and gestured him to keep quiet. "Vivaant, is somebody else coming with you on the trip?" Suvidha asked.

"Yes mom, she is the champion in girls' category. She too won the tickets," said Vivaant.

"And she is our college topper," added one of his friends.

Everyone got down from the cab. Vivaant's friends met Sukheshni and greeted her. She too greeted them and Vivaant's mom and introduced her to Soundarya, her mom.

"Sukheshni, Vivaant told me about you, congrats on being a champion. You are such a brilliant child. He has to learn a lot from you on how to manage sports and studies," Suvidha said.

"Oh! God, Now I have to listen this from my mom too. After I come back, I'll take care of you," Vivaant warned his friend.

Soundarya who was equally worried for her daughter travelling alone was relieved to know that one of her college mates was also going on the same trip to Mt Kailash.

"Vivaant, please take care of Sukheshni and help her when in need," requested Soundarya. Little did she know about the wars that went on between them at college.

"There is no need to worry aunty, I will be there to help," replied Vivaant.

"Sukheshni, please help my son, it's his first trip on a plane," Suvidha requested.

"Don't worry aunty, there will also be the flight crew to help him," Sukheshni assured her.

Vivaant furrowed his eyebrows looking at his mom.

It was 5 a.m. when they entered the airport. The flight was scheduled to leave at 6:30 a.m. The bags were checked at the gate. Sukheshni entered first and proceeded to the check-in counter and a few minutes later Vivaant too entered, but he had no idea what to do.

Vivaant stood there for a few minutes looking here and there while Sukheshni returned with the boarding pass.

Sukheshni teased him, "Oh! Looks like the college champ is lost. Go to the check-in counter over there." She guided him to the check-in counter and asked him to leave his check-in bags there.

It was his first experience in getting into a plane and was thrilled to see the size of it.

There was an announcement made for the passengers travelling towards Lucknow. But lost in his excitement, Vivaant went on to do window shopping at the airport and almost lost his way back.

Somehow, he made it with the help of an aircrew by showing his boarding pass when there were only fifteen minutes left for the plane to take off. He thought he would go and check.

Vivaant's name was being announced for the final call to board the plane. He rushed there and said that he was

Vivaant. "Sir, where were you, we are looking for you from fifteen minutes?" a flight attendant asked him.

He entered the flight and occupied his seat next to Sukheshni who burst out in laughter after hearing his story and assured him that she would try to keep her promise to Suvidha aunty and guide him.

Vivaant felt bit relaxed and happy. This was the first time when they shared a burst of laughter.

She guided him through the Lucknow airport and reached their accommodation organized by Dhithi Research Labs.

"Shall we go and explore Lucknow?" Sukheshni asked Vivaant. She didn't want to waste a single minute of her trip. "Okay, let's get ready fast and meet in half an hour," said Vivaant. Sometime later, they left the hotel and went to visit the zoo and other places in Lucknow.

Dhithi Research Labs

Mr Tarak, the CEO of Dhithi Research Labs was at his office which was nicely set up at the foothills of Mt Kailash, where he had invested the majority of his time researching the wonder, Kailash Parvat.

He sat on his chair thinking about what he would tell the King. Finally, the time was closer to get his hands on the thing he was desperately waiting to get from the last 20 years. Everything was going according to his plan; it was just a matter of time.

It was time to uphold the faith entrusted in him by the council and the King. He bit his nails looking at the clock. He had finished lunch early and come to the office to get his replies ready for the probable questions that the King might pose to him.

He rubbed his hands together looking at the screen waiting for the call that was supposed to come any time now with the King. He got a reminder that the call would start in a few minutes. He went inside the secret meeting room where no one was allowed except him.

Simhanada appeared in a 3D hologram. He was eight feet tall with biceps as rigid as a rock. His mere presence would terrify the people around him. Tarak was one of the shortest of them and was around 5.5 feet tall with a paunch which made it a perfect disguise to live among men.

"Good morning, Tarak," greeted the King.

"Good morning, Your Highness," Tarak bent his knees and continued asking, "For what do I owe this visit, my lord?"

"It's almost ten years here and you have not progressed any further than what it was ten years ago. I'm disappointed," Simhanada said.

"If you are not capable, I shall send someone to replace you." Simhanada added.

"We have got a lead, Your Highness. Our captive is a Mahayogi himself. He has resisted me from entering his mind for almost twenty years." Tarak curled his lips as he continued.

"I have made him weak physically and mentally. With my special ability to read minds I was able to enter his mind and scan his memories and make the dog bark. I was not able to completely see the contents of the box but I have found out where he had hidden the keys, I have made all the arrangements. We should be getting the keys at the earliest.

Once we get hold of the keys, it's just a matter of time that we get hold of the secrets. I will make sure my plan is executed without any hindrance. Please have faith in me, Your Highness, I won't let you down," promised Tarak.

"All the best," was the last sentence from the King before he disconnected the call.

Lucknow Hotel

A car arrived a few meters away from the hotel at Lucknow. Munna and Babloo got down with two of their accomplices and prepared a plan. They wore colourful shirts with long hair and beards with scars on their faces.

"Babloo and I will go upstairs, while the two of you keep the Reception and CCTV persons busy; by which time we will enter their rooms." Munna explained his plan to the team.

Munna and Babloo caught hold of the room service boys and after making them unconscious wore their uniforms and sneaked into the rooms as planned and searched for the pendant and the bracelet in their bags, wardrobes and bathrooms but they could not find anything which matched the description given to them.

"A small blue colour sword-shaped pendant with 7 coloured stones on it and a blue stone bracelet with 7 colour stones." They had got a clear description of the things they were looking for.

They knew their boss wouldn't be happy with their work, but they were running out of time. Before anyone could find out what happened to the room service boys, they had to get out.

"Sir, we searched all over the rooms but could not find the pendant and bracelet," Munna called Tarak and informed him.

Tarak collapsed into a chair clutching at himself. "That's just what I needed today! Another disappointment, where will they go? They are coming here to me. I will take care of them once they enter Tibetan land."

Sukheshni and Vivaant returned after spending a wonderful time together at the zoo. Ragging one another and recalling their college days about how they used to quarrel with each other like small kids. Vivaant saw some old people begging for food on the road while going to have snacks at a restaurant. Vivaant purchased some food packets and handed it over to the old people on the road. They blessed him to be happy and healthy forever.

Sukheshni's heart melted by looking at the scene and she said, "I never knew this side of you."

"It's nothing, these people have been deserted by their families and I have endured that pain all my life. So I try helping such people as much I can," explained Vivaant.

As they entered the hotel, the receptionist looking worried came towards them and said that some thieves had broken into their rooms and they didn't know what they had taken.

They found out that two of their employees were unconscious after some time. "You both can stay here in the rooms next to the reception on the ground floor and we assure you that your security will be taken care of," said the receptionist.

They both went and checked their rooms, but it looked like nothing was stolen but everything was scattered. Later their luggage was shifted to the rooms on the ground floor.

They couldn't sleep the whole night thinking about the incident. They got ready early next morning for their trip to Darchula which was 14-15 hours' drive in an AC bus with other tourists who had come on Kailash Parikrama. Vivaant and Sukheshni were excited and yet worried about what had happened.

The bus left Lucknow at 7 a.m., but it was late when they reached Darchula. They got a place to stay and some good local food and then they rested for the night.

The next day they visited Narayan ashram where they met some yogis on their trip to Kailash. They were guided by a person called Kanha. All the yogis were taking rest as their trek was exhaustive. Some yogis were injured while trekking on the steep mountains.

Kanha was wearing a maroon robe like the monks and was always there to help the yogis. He was active and patiently listened to each of their needs and queries and made them feel comfortable.

Vivaant was inspired by observing elderly people who were walking on the path to Kailash and was astonished at their fitness levels. Kanha was motivating and guiding them.

"Hi, I am Vivaant. I am amazed at seeing these yogis. How come they are so fit and where are they headed?

Where are you guiding them to?" asked Vivaant after introducing himself to Kanha.

"Hi Vivaant, I am Kanha, I am not a guide. I have my small business setup here. I am doing my humble duty of being a good citizen. As a youth, it's my duty to help elderly persons," replied Kanha.

Vivaant joined Kanha to help the monks climb the mountain and provided first aid to the injured. Sukheshni observed the manner in which they cared for the elderly persons and served them water.

Kanha thanked Vivaant and bade him farewell as the yogis were ready to start their trip and hoped they would meet soon.

Vivaant, Sukheshni and their group finally arrived at Sirkha where they were spending the night.

Dhithi Research Labs

Devaant, Tarak's son was taking over the responsibilities from his father and provided some relief to him from office work of Dhithi Research Labs. His enthusiasm for sports had led him to set up Dhithi Sports Academy.

Devaant had his interest in sports and he used to play Cricket and Football with friends whenever possible. He had a dream of building the biggest sports centre in the world with indoor cricket and football stadiums at different levels. He was well above 6 ft. He always wore suits and goggles. His friends used to comment that - suits suit no one like they suit him.

Devaant was also overseeing the research being carried out near Mt Kailash. Researchers had found some new metals and stones. Scientists were researching the new stones which emitted some sort of radiation.

Devaant was always fascinated growing up on the foothills of Mt Kailash seeing such a serene place holding secrets for which his father was desperately after. Stories he had heard about Mt Kailash in the religious scriptures of Hindus, Jains and Bons made him intensely inquisitive about the secret.

He was keen to know about the secrets the box held within. It was locked by some sort of a mechanism.

He knew from his father that the keys were with Vivaant and Sukheshni. He had told his team that he needed the keys at any cost. He had directed his team to keep a tab on them and if they couldn't retrieve the keys, they had to kidnap them and bring them to him.

Sirkha

"From here the trek starts. There are thousands of steps which are formed by rocky boulders. We have to tread carefully. It will be difficult to trek at this height. Please take care of yourselves and help the elderly," the guide addressed the people who had come for the Kailash trip.

Everybody was given proper training by the guide who took them on a short acclimatization trip. The team finished their trip and returned to the tents.

It was evening and everyone was tired from the trek and went to take rest after a cup of refreshing tea. Vivaant and Sukheshni saw the fireflies and enjoyed the view in the cold weather.

A Fire Camp was set-up later in the evening. The guide invited the couples to dance and entertain themselves. All the couples were having a great time in the romantic environment. Taking turns, they started dancing to the music. Loud speakers played romantic Hindi songs. It was Vivaant's turn, and he couldn't dance for the lack of a partner. However, the elders present there coaxed Sukheshni to dance with him.

Vivaant and Sukheshni went in to dance holding each other in a salsa pose. Snowflakes and fireflies made it resemble a dance floor. They were slowly moving their legs following the others and looking deeply into each other's eyes. It was as if two dolls were dancing inside a snow glass globe. It looked magical. Claps after the song broke their eye contact.

Sukheshni called Vivaant for a walk after dinner when everyone went to sleep. They both put on their jackets and went out for a short walk.

"It's such cold weather and these snowflakes and fireflies are making it look beautiful. The best thing about these places is you can view all the stars up there and I always remember the Orion constellation, the most easily recognizable one. In Bangalore, you cannot even see a star," remarked Vivaant.

"Yes, my mother used to tell me, when we were in Madikeri and I was a small kid. Whenever I used to cry my dad used to take me outside to show me the stars and I used to keep quiet. That is the only memory I have about my dad," said Sukheshni.

"I also do not have any memory of my father. I don't even remember seeing his face." Vivaant was talking but

Sukheshni was looking at the sky remembering her father and walked a few steps and fell down a steep cliff.

"Help!!! Help!!!" Sukheshni cried while sliding down the steep cliff.

Vivaant kept on calling out her name for a few minutes. He didn't know what to do when he didn't get any response to his shouts. So, he too started sliding down the cliff, the way Sukheshni had gone down.

After a while, he found a road. He was searching for her and calling out her name on that road. He saw a Jeep with armed men carrying her.

For a minute he felt that some terrorists might be kidnapping her. He ran behind the Jeep but couldn't catch up with it. However, he saw her lying unconscious in the Jeep.

He tried to get help. Finally, he found a guy standing on the side of the road and relieving himself against a wall. He saw his bike parked on the side, and without wasting a moment, he started the bike and followed the Jeep, ignoring the bike owner's plea to stop the bike.

He saw the Jeep entering the military camp and noticed the logo of the Indian Army and was finally relieved, but as he had entered without permission he was arrested.

Vivaant was presented before the higher officials in the army. He explained that he came looking for his friend, Sukheshni and they were on their trek to Kailash Parikrama and had reached Sirkha and showed his ID.

The officer was convinced and led him to the medical camp where they were treating Sukheshni as she had minor injuries. She was happy on seeing Vivaant there and told him that she had fallen and asked him how he found her and how he got those injuries. He narrated what had happened and finally got some treatment for his injuries. The officer asked them to leave early the next morning before the Colonel arrived.

Sukheshni asked Vivaant as to why he had taken the risk of falling off the cliff than getting some help.

Vivaant said, "I was keeping myself up the promise I had made to your mother to take care of you."

The next day at 5 a.m. when they were preparing to leave with some sepoys in a Jeep, the Colonel entered the camp. He enquired about them and ordered them to be presented in his office.

Sukheshni and Vivaant entered the Colonel's office. Tears welled up in Sukheshni's eyes as she saw her father's photo framed in his office. She was instantly pulled towards the photo frame and she started crying and slowly whispered, "Dad!"

Colonel Veerprathap Singh looked at the scene and it took a few seconds for him to realize that she was the daughter of his dear old friend, Late Lieutenant Ponnappa.

A memory flashed across the Colonel's mind when he was playing with Ponnappa's daughter on a visit to their house long ago.

The Colonel invited them to be seated and asked Sukheshni about how they landed there and Vivaant narrated their adventure to the Colonel.

"How is your mother Sukheshni? Where is your family located now?" the Colonel enquired.

Both of them had ignored Vivaant and were sharing a wonderful father and daughter moment. The Colonel knew that she never had got a chance to spend her childhood with her father.

The Colonel's eye quickly noticed the silver chain with a blue pendant which Vivaant was wearing.

"Who is your father boy?" asked the Colonel.

"I don't want to talk about him. He is nobody either to me or my family. He had abandoned me and my mother when I was a little boy," Vivaant replied.

"Is your father Dr Vishwanath?" The Colonel smiled and asked.

Vivaant looked puzzled as did Sukheshni. He was wondering how he knew about his father and what connection he had with him.

He had never even mentioned his father's name in the last few years and yet here was a stranger who recognized him with his father's name.

"Yes," Vivaant replied with wide eyes, not knowing what to say further. He didn't even want to ask about his father but was still curious about how the Colonel knew him. Taking them to the Cafeteria, the Colonel said, "Let us talk over breakfast and by the way, you guys inform your team that you are safe with the Indian Army and will come after a while."

They served themselves aloo parathas and pieces of bread and sat at a table. The cafeteria was empty as the soldiers were yet to arrive for their breakfast as they were engaged in training and exercises.

"Ponnappa and I had set up this camp twenty years ago. Later the Government of India sent an archaeological team to survey Mt Kailash, and it was headed by Dr Vishwanath. He had come here on an assignment to explore Mt Kailash and found out some important things." The Colonel started remembering the past and narrated it to Vivaant and Sukheshni.

"We had already told them that many other people were trying to explore Mt Kailash and might harm our archaeological team. We were then asked to provide protection to Dr Vishwanath and his team from their evil eyes.

After a few months of research, he informed us that some guys possessing weapons and accompanied by a few people were looking for something and they had threatened our archaeological team to leave the place.

Sukheshni's father and I tried to follow them. Initially we didn't find any clue but finally, after following them for a few days we found out that they must have some link to Dhithi Research Lab.

With the security provided by us; Dr Vishwanath was finally able to start his excavation. One fine day while excavating, Dr Vishwanath found a Treasure Box. The Colonel showed them the drawing of the Treasure Box.

The name Dhithi Research Lab rang a bell in Sukheshni and Vivaant's minds, but they kept quiet.

"Before coming here, Lieutenant Ponnappa and your father were amazed by what they had found and were scared. The other excavators were following them to get their hands on that box.

Ponnappa had kept them away and brought the box and Dr Vishwanath to safety. Vishwanath had said that he had locked it and wanted to keep the box in a safe place and even if they found it, he had ensured that they couldn't open it.

They took the pendant and stones out of the secret box. They went to their respective hometowns and hid it there and told me that they would reveal what was in the box once they return. As they were in a hurry, I did not bother them much.

I last saw the pendant that you are wearing now when your father went to his hometown. I noticed in the coming weeks that a few people were watching over our camp. We had increased our security." The Colonel tried to explain the position of Dr Vishwanath to Vivaant.

"Is that the time when my dad returned with my brother and left me and my mom back home? Did something happen to my father after he came back here?" Vivaant asked.

"Yes, unfortunately," the Colonel continued, "after a few weeks, Dr Vishwanath returned with your brother Vedaant; and Ponnappa had already returned by that time. Dr Vishwanath shared that he had a rough time at home and had a fight with your mother and your grandparents for not being available most of the year and at the time of your birth she had to take care of two small kids.

Your grandparents wanted him to take his wife and kids with him, they didn't understand why he didn't want the family here. Vishwanath didn't want to tell your mom about the dangers he was exposed to here because it would scare her and she would not let him return.

He tried convincing them in other ways but there was no one to support him. So, at night he took your brother and thought he would admit him to a boarding school here and came to Sirkha."

"After that what happened was the worst evening of my life." With tears rolling down his eyes, the Colonel remembering that night recounted to Vivaant and Sukheshni as to what had happened.

Sukheshni's eyes filled up with love for her dad. She stood up, with her chin high, looking at her father's picture after listening to the story of valor that her father had displayed.

After a brief pause, the Colonel continued, "Dr Vishwanath and Vedaant were nowhere to be found. They might have been kidnapped along with the box."

The Colonel looked at Vivaant who was trying to stop his tears from his wet eyes for what all he knew and imagined about his father was wrong. His father loved him and his mother unlike his imagination.

"Your father didn't abandon you, my child, he was taken away with your brother." The Colonel said looking at Vivaant.

"We tried a lot to find them but could not. After a few days we got news about a dead body of a 4-5-year-old kid found in Tibet. I did not inform your mother. I thought it would be better for her to live with the thought of an abandoned husband than a kidnapped husband and a dead son.

We found some clues that pointed towards Tarak and Dhithi Research Labs. But our hands were tied as it was on Tibetan soil and we didn't have a good relationship with the Chinese Government. There is still tension at the border and our military operations are confined till the Indian boundary."

"Isn't it the same Dhithi Research Labs that has sponsored our trip?" asked Sukheshni looking at Vivaant and the Colonel.

"Yes, my ears twitched when you guys told me that your trip was sponsored by Dhithi Research Labs. I smelt something fishy about how you both are sponsored and brought here at the same time.

But you told us there are twenty other people with you guys, so that should not be an issue. Have you guys informed them? "the Colonel asked.

"Yes, they are waiting for us at the starting point of the trek," Vivaant replied. He was still trying to comprehend the truth about his father.

"Nothing to worry. We have one of our spies, a RAW agent, Kanhaiya, who is working on Tibetan soil for us to help and investigate Dhithi Research Labs.

Take this card, this has his number; call him once you reach your hotel at Burang and be in touch with him. He will look after you guys if Tarak tries to do anything nasty. I will talk to him and inform him to keep an eye on both of you." The Colonel handed over the card to Vivaant and told them to take care of themselves.

"Thanks Sir," Vivaant asked permission to leave. His mind was now filled with hundreds of questions. "Where were his father and brother? Why were they kidnapped? What was in that Treasure box? What are these Keys? What is the role of Dhithi Research Labs?" The only person who would have any information about this would be the RAW agent, Kanhaiya. Vivaant wanted to meet him in Tibet and ask all these questions.

Colonel Veerprathap Singh ordered his driver to drop them at the starting point of the trek.

Around 12 noon, they joined their trek team at Sirkha. The guide and most of them were worried. They were missing since last night and they were looking for them frantically from 5 a.m.

They went to take rest in their rooms after narrating what had happened. The guide was extremely upset until Vivaant had called and conveyed that they were safe with the Indian Army.

The guide and others observed that both had some injuries, so they advised them to take rest till evening and they would commence the trek the following day.

The next day morning they left for Gala village. It was a beautiful trek of the big green mountains with varieties of trees and waterfalls and the scenic backdrop of the snowy mountains of the Himalayas.

They met many villagers on the way and came to know about the local culture and tradition. People wore colourful robes which was their local dress. They took pictures along with them.

They were served with mouthwatering rotis and sabzi with pudina chutney for lunch at a village.

They came across the flora and fauna of the forest region. They were lucky enough to see cobra lilies the flowers in the shape of a snake which was very attractive.

The guide showed them the medicinal plants which had leaves with thorns and said it would act as a pain reliever for knee pain.

The next day after taking rest at the Gala village, the team left for Bodhi. Most of them were relieved that they had to go down 4,000 steps to reach Bodhi.

On the way, they found an amazing waterfall where everyone could spend time and they had a bath and refreshed themselves.

The army jawans, Vivaant and Sukheshni helped the elderly people to go down the steps and walk on the rough roads and the team reached Lakhanpur to have their meals by which time, everyone was tired.

Moving forward they reached Malpa where 300 people had died in a tragic flood and landslide a few years ago. They were accompanied on their journey by the beautiful and roaring Kaali river and they finally reached Bodhi village and set up tents and camped there for the night.

As everyone's eyes were closing involuntarily they went and had a sound sleep as they had to wake up early the next morning.

The next day they reached Gunji through Garbayang, where they had a medical checkup at the ITBP camp. They had training from the commandant who was the liaison officer.

From Gunji an army truck ferried them to Kaalapaani which was 9 kms away, the starting point of the Kaali river and they then visited the Ved Vyas cave.

There were trees all over the forest which were used to make paper called Bhojpatra during the Vedic period.

Everyone finished filling their immigration forms to enter Tibetan land governed by China. After walking for a short distance, they were able to see the OM Parvat, which was a marvel in itself and they then reached Navidhang. They were amazed to see such facilities built and provided by ITBP at such a high altitude.

They left Navidhang at the unearthly hour of 2 a.m. It was freezing cold and many were facing difficulty in breathing. Vivaant and a few ITBP jawans helped those who faced difficulty in breathing.

By 7 a.m. they reached the Lipulek pass and the ITBP jawans had cautioned them that if they delayed, the snow would start melting and it would be tough for them to pass.

Everyone was handed over to the care of the Chinese army who checked their passports and immigration papers. After another two kms, a bus was booked for the tourists which took them to Burang Hotel and they rested there before proceeding further.

Chapter 2

DAYS AT GURUJI'S ASHRAM

Burang Hotel

The next day was spent in customs and immigration check and later everyone in the hotel went shopping in the afternoon. Vivaant and Sukheshni finished their shopping and returned to the hotel. Their room was on the first floor and the whole floor was empty. No one had returned from shopping yet.

They heard some noise coming from their rooms. Vivaant motioned Sukheshni to remain quiet. He went near the room and heard someone talking loudly. Initially, he thought it might be someone from room service. He went closer to the room and stood near the door listening to what they were speaking.

"Call Devaant Sir and inform him about this," Wangmo instructed Dorjee. Speaking on the phone, Dorjee said, "Sir, we didn't find the blue pendant or the blue bracelet. I think they might have taken it with them."

"I will send some backup and photos of those guys. As soon as they reach the hotel kidnap them and bring them to me," Devaant replied over the phone.

"Sure sir, we will wait outside the hotel and as soon as they arrive, we will bring them to you." Dorjee replied.

Hearing them Vivaant's heart started racing with fear. He looked at Sukheshni in shock and quickly signaled her to hide behind the first-floor reception counter.

Vivaant joined her and both of them hid behind the reception counter and he gestured her not to make any sound. As soon as Dorjee and Wangmo left the room and went down, Vivaant checked through the window and saw them walking towards the parking lot.

Vivaant and Sukheshni went to their respective rooms and to their dismay they found their things scattered all over. They knew they were in a perilous situation.

Sukheshni's sweat started to drip down from her forehead, "Are we going to be kidnapped? Shall we call the police? Call Reception and tell them?"

"Don't worry I will figure it out, don't get tensed. Even if we get out of this situation now, Dhithi Research Labs would have set traps for us even in the coming days; they have sponsored this trip and booked these hotels. Let's call Kanhaiya, the RAW agent who was referred by Colonel Veerprathap Singh," Vivaant convinced Sukheshni.

He quickly called Kanhaiya. "Hello Sir, I am Vivaant. Colonel Veerprathap Singh might have told you about us. We are in a hotel at Burang. We are in grave danger. Some guys have come to kidnap us. I heard them talking. They are waiting outside at the parking lot. We don't know what to do. We are scared."

"Don't worry, I will help you. I will come near the parking lot of the hotel in my Jeep. I will take 15-20 mins to reach and by that time you guys somehow come in disguise and fool them and get into my Jeep. I will take you to a safe place." Kanhaiya cautioned them after hearing Vivaant and gave him the Jeep's number.

Vivaant and Sukheshni packed some of their important things and clothes in a small bag in spite of Sukheshni's resistance. They tried to fit both their clothes in one single bag as Vivaant knew she couldn't run fast with bags if they were chased.

Sukheshni had an idea. "I will dress up like a man with your clothes and you dress up like a woman so that we can quickly pass through the parking lot without getting noticed to the main road where Kanhaiya said he'd be waiting for us."

Vivaant knew it would look stupid but did not have any time to think about other options and so he agreed to the plan in that situation and put on Sukheshni's clothes and she put on his dress and jackets. Sukheshni applied some makeup on Vivaant to make him resemble a woman.

Twenty minutes later, Vivaant called Kanhaiya again from the hotel. "We are ready." "I have come near the main road; you guys somehow come near the Jeep. Take your time, I will be waiting." Kanhaiya instructed Vivaant.

Vivaant and Sukheshni took their small bag and went outside the hotel and silently walked towards the main road. Dorjee who was sitting on his Jeep juggling around his Jeep keys observed the bags and realized those were the same bags which they had checked an hour earlier and they belonged to Vivaant and Sukheshni.

Dorjee shouted at Wangmo, "Catch them; he is carrying the bag we just checked." They both ran towards Vivaant and Sukheshni.

Kanhaiya started the Jeep and Vivaant and Sukheshni jumped into it and Kanhaiya drove quickly towards Darchen. Dorjee and Wangmo chased them in their Jeep.

"Below your seat, there are belts with nails which can puncture their Jeep's tyres. Pick them and aim it at their tyres," instructed Kanhaiya.

Vivaant and Sukheshni took those belts with some sharp nails embedded. "Slow down Kanhaiya," said Vivaant, "let them come near and we can aim better." As they came near both aimed at the Jeep's tyres and threw the belts.

Dorjee lost control of his Jeep as the tyres were punctured and they had to stop and curse themselves as they could not get hold of Vivaant and Sukheshni.

Vivaant looked at Kanhaiya and said, "So, Kanha you are an Indian spy." Kanhaiya was surprised as to how he was addressing him by his nickname.

He turned and saw Vivaant when he removed the scarf which he wore around his head. Kanha realized he was the same boy whom he had met at Narayan Ashram and burst out in laughter.

"Yes, I am and you are looking beautiful in this outfit," Kanha teased Vivaant.

"I told you, it was your idea to make me look ridiculous. All this for nothing. They recognized us anyway," Vivaant nagged Sukheshni.

"It was because of me, we got away. Now don't say it was for nothing. Else we could not have reached till the Jeep also," argued Sukheshni.

"It's okay guys, settle it. It's good news that you are safe. I will take you to a safe place," said Kanha and stopped their argument.

Kanha drove them to the ashram where all yogis whom he had accompanied were staying. Kanha said that it was his residential quarters as it was the perfect place to be undercover among yogis and carry out his operations.

"Someshwara Guruji is knowledgeable and you could also learn a few things from him. I'll speak to Guruji. You guys can stay here till we arrange your safe passage to India as it is dangerous here now. Use my room and please change your getups first. I will meet you after speaking to Guruji about your accommodation," Kanha said with a giggle seeing Vivaant's makeup.

Vivaant raised one of his eyebrows and looked up and started to think. It was certain that they were looking for his pendant but what were they looking for in Sukheshni's room?

"Sukheshni, do you also have a pendant which your father gave to your mother?" Vivaant asked Sukheshni.

She opened her bag and showed a lucky bracelet which was made up of blue spherical stones and some coloured stones. "No, not a pendant. I have this bracelet which was given to my mom by my father. I usually wear this bracelet all the time. Maybe that's what brought me here." Sukheshni told him.

"My mom also would give it to me to wear on most of the occasions during exams and outings. Maybe somebody was watching us while we were in Bangalore and sponsored us to come over here!" Vivaant gasped.

He was surprised to see Sukheshni's bracelet had the same rainbow coloured stones which were on his pendant and the other stones too were made up of the same blue stone which his pendant was made up of.

Now he was sure they were looking for this blue colour stone pendant and the bracelet for something.

Kanha came back and guided them towards a small room in the ashram where they were permitted to stay. Sukheshni stayed there and Kanha took Vivaant to his room. After taking rest for an hour, Sukheshni came to Kanha's room.

Vivaant narrated to Kanha as to what all had happened from the starting at Lucknow Hotel and he could make out that everyone was in search of the pendant and the bracelet.

"I know about the secret box, Colonel Veerprathap Singh had explained to me what had happened to both your fathers after the secret box was hidden. My gut feeling says that you have got the pendant and the stones of the bracelet that might be from the box," said Kanha and continued.

"When your fathers returned to their homes, they gave it to your mothers and when they returned, Dr Vishwanath and Vedaant were kidnapped and Lieutenant Ponnappa was martyred." Kanha summarized.

Vivaant agreed and said, "I think the pendant and bracelet might be some sort of a key to open the secret box which Dhithi Research Labs might already have acquired and that might contain something precious. They are eager to get their hands on it. So, they had planned it and sponsored our trips."

"Do you know what happened to my father after he was kidnapped by people at Dhithi Research Labs? Do you know if he is still alive? " Vivaant asked Kanha as he could not wait long enough to ask these questions.

"I know the kidnapping was carried out by Tarak, the CEO of Dhithi Research Labs but nothing more than that. Until now they were not active on this issue but now we can resume our work. Don't worry, if I get a chance, I will certainly try to rescue your father." Kanha assured Vivaant.

Everybody pondered over these happenings and went to dinner at prasadalaya. Vivaant and Kanha volunteered to serve food at the prasadalaya to the yogis and Guruji was happy to see them serving the food.

Guruji was watching over the proceedings and asked Vivaant and Kanha to have their meals after serving the others. After their meals, they went for a short walk across the field in the ashram.

"From tomorrow a session will be starting on how life on Earth came into existence and it will be a great session and you can ask any questions to Guruji about it if you want," Kanha informed Vivaant and Sukheshni.

"Sounds interesting, I will be waiting for it. I am interested but never got a chance to attend seminars like this," Vivaant said excitedly.

"Before that, you wake up early and get ready for the Yoga session. So, take rest now," Kanha advised them.

Vivaant and Sukheshni called their mothers from Kanha's mobile and conveyed everything was fine with the trip and going as per plan. They made sure their mothers believed they were safe. They then retired to their rooms.

Vivaant woke up early the next morning and got ready. He was keen to attend the day's discussion. Vivaant and Sukheshni participated in the yoga sessions, enjoyed the fresh air in the morning and did pranayama and sun salutations. After that, they freshened up and had breakfast.

Everyone assembled at the discussion hall and sat with the other yogis. There was pin-drop silence when Guruji entered. He sat on a chair on the stage. Guruji greeted everyone and said that they would all chant OM thrice.

Guruji spoke. "As you all might be aware, today we are going to discuss on how, as we know, life came into existence on Earth and how we are still living on this planet even after so many disasters. Floods happened on Earth and wiped out life and we hear some history of our ancestors from the ancient texts.

I will try to share my experience and knowledge that I have gained through my research and speaking with other intellectuals. I spend most of the time meditating and focusing on the energy which runs the whole universe and cosmos, the Mahavishnu who rests in the cosmic ocean."

Vivaant initially felt that this would be like any other speech by other gurus about god but he hoped he would be proved wrong.

Someshwara Guruji spoke by praying to Mahavishnu.

"I bow to Mahavishnu who rests in the cosmic ocean and creates these bubbles called universes. Each of these bubbles is a parallel universe.

Each universe has many galaxies like our own Milky Way which was created by our Brahma. Each galaxy has its architect in Brahma. Each universe has similar creations, but might not be in the same situation as we are.

Brahma stays on his planet called Satya Loka at the centre of the Milky Way. Our Solar System revolves around Brahma Loka in a spiral manner around the Milky Way once every 260 million years, which is one year of Brahma. The lifespan of the Milky Way is 26 billion years. According to research, the current age of the Milky Way is 13.1 billion years and our ancient Hindu texts say that this is the 51st year of Brahma. He has completed half of his life span, i.e., 13 billion years.

Visual of the Satya Loka spiral and the asteroid belt

I will share some important facts which are found by recent studies that for every 26 million years, the Solar System travels around the asteroid belt of the galactic centre and scientists have found that they could trace mass extinctions for every 26 million years. In one of those catastrophic events, Dinosaurs became extinct on this planet.

Like Brahma has his own planet called Satya Loka, there are 14 lokas in which beings live and as explained in Hindu, Jain and other religious texts, there are seven lokas above and seven lokas below us." Guruji explained about the 14 lokas.

1. Satya Loka - Where the supreme consciousness Brahma lives.
2. Tapo Loka - Where the immortal beings live, they have supreme knowledge and access to Satya Loka.
3. Jana Loka - Where the realized souls live, they have complete access to the material world.
4. Mahar Loka - Where great sages live. They go through severe penance and have achieved supreme powers and knowledge which they transmit to the lower lokas.
5. Swarga Loka - Where the Devas and Gandharvas live. They try to control the lower lokas.
6. Bhuvar Loka - Where the Danavas live.
7. Bhu Loka - Where we human beings live.
8. Atal Loka – The underground city below Bhu Loka, ruled by Bala, the son of Maya.
9. Vitala Loka - The underground city where beings lead their lives mining gold.
10. Sutala Loka - The underground city ruled by King Bali.
11. Talatala Loka - The underground city where the architect, Maya rules.
12. Mahatala Loka - The underground city where hooded Nagas exist.
13. Rasatala Loka - The underground city where the Daityas live.
14. Patala Loka - The underground city where Nagas with many hoods live. It is ruled by the Naga King, Vasuki.

Vivaant looked lost in the imaginary world of all lokas in his head and wasastonished by the amount of knowledge Guruji had about astrophysics and recent discoveries published in research papers and other publications and what made him special was that he was able to relate it to ancient Hindu texts and explain them.

Guruji left for a break and said that they could discuss more in the next session.

"How did Guruji gain so much knowledge?" Vivaant asked Kanhaiya.

"Being in the mountains and staying away from all the advanced cities does not mean he is away from all the discoveries and research going on. Many scientists come here to debate and acquire knowledge from Guruji," Kanhaiya replied.

Guruji started the second session by chanting OM and everyone followed.

Vivaant was now engrossed in Guruji's speech and was attentive with eyes wide open.

Guruji started his session by saying - "Everything in the universe revolves first around itself and then revolves around another thing and always moving in forward pace in an ever-expanding universe until one day it contracts and returns to the starting point.

Earth revolves around its tilted axis. Once every 2,160 years it shifts from one zodiac constellation to another and finishes a circle of 12 zodiac constellations for 25,920 years, this is called precession or Plutonian year.

One more thought-provoking thing to observe is the Sun completing an elliptical path around its binary star Sirius which is a bigger star than our Sun and it takes exactly the same amount of time, i.e., 25,920 years.

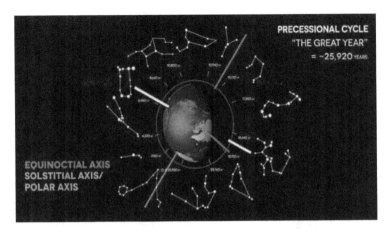

Vivaant remembered a similar speech he had heard on YouTube about a year back and he had followed up with many more videos on yugas.

Guruji continued, "There will be a question and answer session now. If anyone has any questions to ask, now is the time."

"I have seen some videos on YouTube. There was a mention in the speech that the Sun revolves around a super sun and one revolution around the super sun constitutes one yuga cycle. Is it the same cycle that you were speaking about?" asked Vivaant.

Guruji replied, "Yes my child you are correct. Why don't you share my load and speak to the audience about what all you have learned over the internet? I can correct you if you are wrong. This is a great platform to share your knowledge with all the yogis and then I will continue."

Guruji invited Vivaant on to the stage. Vivaant went up to the podium and greeted everyone with a namaskar.

"As Guruji mentioned, the Sun and Sirius revolve around one another in a binary star system," Vivaant started his speech.

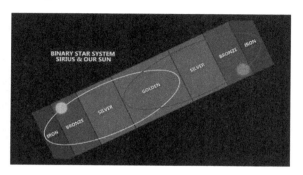

A visual of the Sun and Sirius in binary system

"And the Earth revolving around itself to complete its axis by revolving around all the 12 constellations also takes 25,920 years which also makes one yuga cycle of all four yugas in ascending and descending order. If we divide it into half it becomes 12,960 years.

He drew a diagram on the board and explained to the audience the 12,960 years of a descending yuga and another cycle of ascending yuga.

"When we divide these yugas in 4:3:2:1 ratio, we can deduce that 5,184 years of Satyayuga and 3,888 years of Tretayuga and 2,592 years of Dwaparayuga and Kaliyuga for 1,296 years.

Descending yugas show the decline of human technological and spiritual knowledge as they move away from the Super Sun which is the Sirius star and the endpoint where the Sun and Sirius were far from each other was in 1806 BC if we consider BC and AD for reference.

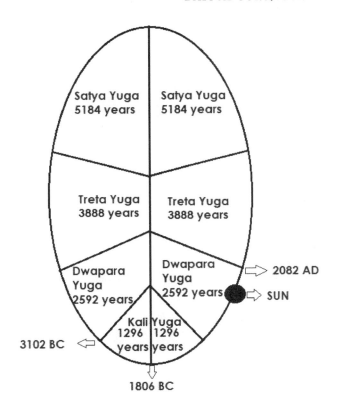

Human intelligence, technological advancements, and average human lifespan were at a peak low. If we read our history carefully, we see that the average human lifespan was 20-30 years because plague prevailed all over the world.

Our ancient texts or epics mention that we were considering 3102 BC as Krishna's life on Earth which was the end of Dwaparayuga. 1,296 years after that was 1806 BC, the end of descending Kaliyuga and the ascending Kaliyuga started.

The Srimad Bhagavatam mentions:

tatas canu-dinam dharmah
satyam saucam kshamadaya
kalena balina rajan
nanksysty ayur balam smrtih

– Srimad Bhagavatam, 12.2.1

It says the process of age, Kaliyuga dharma, religious principles, truthfulness, cleanliness, forgiveness, mercifulness, duration of life, bodily strength, memory, etc., will all diminish day-by-day in Kaliyuga.

By looking at our present, do we still feel this is Kaliyuga? One's life expectancy is increasing every day due to medical advancements, we treat everyone equal, we maintain cleanliness and our memory is increasing generation after generation. With that I can conclude that we are in ascending order of yugas, we have passed Kaliyuga.

We can also see that when we were approaching the end of ascending Kaliyuga around 510 BC many great souls like Buddha and Mahavir showed us the way to attain salvation.

And now we are in Dwaparayuga. In 2082 AD we will move ahead in our spiritual thinking and technological advancements as we move forward towards Sirius.

And while reading other research papers published by the Indian Institute of Scientific Research on Vedas about Mahabharat and Ramayana; astronomical dating by Skyview, the software tells us the dates of the Ramayana and the Mahabharata." Vivaant concluded his speech by saying this is what he had learned from doing research on the internet with his limited understanding.

"But I still have so many questions on my mind about why we only have knowledge of our current cycle of yugas. What about the cycles beyond that? Was astronomical dating so perfect those days and is the science behind this astrology true?" Vivaant stopped and looked at Guruji.

Guruji smiled and replied, "You indeed have done a lot of research and know a lot, my child. You have eased a lot of my work. Let us all meet after lunch and talk more about it."

Kanha joined Vivaant in serving food to all the yogis and told him he had done a lot of research on this. I didn't know you had so much interest in all of this.

They served food to all the yogis along with a few more volunteers and then had their meals and went back to the hall where Guruji was meditating silently.

After everybody came back and settled down, Guruji chanted OM. Everyone followed and then Guruji exchanged pleasantries.

Starting the third session Guruji said, "It was a motivating session we had. Vivaant raised some interesting questions like what had happened before Satyayuga and why do we not know about history beyond that?

There is a hard truth we should all know that life on Earth is short compared to that of the life span of the universe. The life span of human life is over 100 years at the maximum.

Life on the landmass of the Earth will vanish after every 25,920 years. This one cycle of yuga is called Manvantara

- the life span of a generation of Manu or in the west as he is called Adam.

But it isn't the end of life on Earth. There are far more intelligent species like Reptilian or as we call them Nagas who live in underground cities and Mermen and Mermaids or as you guys know as your favourite hero Aquaman lives in oceans, usually survives these catastrophic events. Nagas have their own marvellous underground cities and live in them because they know that life on the landmass vanishes for every 25,920 years."

"If you have any questions please ask now, so that we can discuss them tomorrow." Guruji told the gathering.

Vivaant questioned Guruji, "But how do we know that for 25,920 years this cycle of extinction happens? "

Guruji replied, "Let's talk about that in tomorrow's session. Now let's do some meditation and pranayama and end the session."

Dhithi Research Labs

Devaant threw things on his table, he knew he had to face his father empty-handed which he never liked. "You guys are the biggest failures; I don't know why I still entrust you guys with such work. You could not even get small keys or get those kids who are in our territory. You guys are losers and you are trying to make me one. I will give you one last chance to go and find them and bring them to me or else there won't be a second chance this time."

Mr Tarak was disappointed that Devaant could not execute his plan and they were still not able to get their hands on the pendant and the bracelet to open the secret chest which they were yet to open. Tarak wanted to give another chance to Devaant to see his potential.

Mr Tarak only wanted it to open the right way, he did not want to break it even though Devaant insisted on breaking it.

"What was there in the chest which was so important that Tarak wouldn't even risk breaking it open?" Devaant always wondered.

Dorjee and Wangmo came up with a piece of news. "We have enquired about the Jeep that rescued Vivaant and Sukheshni. We got information from a local garage that a guy usually brings in the Jeep for a checkup once a week. The garage guy Dawa said that he would call them the next time when he turns in with the Jeep," Dorjee informed Devaant at their office.

"Go catch him and find out where those kids are. Bring them to me." Devaant thundered at Dorjee and Wangmo.

Kanhaiya had to take some important calls regarding the recent happenings. So, he left the ashram saying that he would be back by night.

Kanhaiya called the garage guy to tell him that he was coming over to get some tinkering done in the shop.

"That guy is going to come with his Jeep to the shop tomorrow for some tinkering," Dawa informed Dorjee.

Dorjee and Wangmo rushed to the garage and hid inside waiting for Kanhaiya.

Kanhaiya came to the garage and recognized the Jeep standing outside was of the two criminals whom he had seen in the hotel's parking lot.

Kanhaiya quickly implanted a GPS tracking device on Dorjee's Jeep and informed his team to track its location.

Kanhaiya knew he was in for some exciting action inside the garage. He was a well-trained RAW agent with some cool spy gadgets.

As he entered the garage with his Jeep, Dawa came and greeted him. "Hello sir, what work do I need to do?"

Kanhaiya saw two guys close to the door of the garage. Dorjee and Wangmo clapped their hands.

"So, you think you are some kind of a Superhero, who can come and save anyone in danger?" Dorjee chuckled.

"If you still doubt it, come and try me," invited Kanha.

Wangmo came charging at Kanha who quickly took out his pen which turned into a sharp-edged small knife and threw it at Wangmo's leg. Wangmo fell as his leg started bleeding badly.

Dorjee charged at him with an iron rod in his hand. Kanhaiya bent falling backwards and dodged the first hit, quickly rolled towards his right and caught hold of a spanner and aimed it right at Dorjee's hand resulting in the iron rod falling to the ground.

When Dorjee bent back to take the iron rod, Kanhaiya rolled back to his left and kicked right in the face of Dorjee and quickly got up and gave a sharp elbow blow to Dorjee's face. Dorjee's mouth filled with blood as he fell on the ground on his back.

Wangmo was bleeding from his right leg badly after the knife cut. Kanhaiya went near him, collected his knife and asked him to get it treated and tell his boss to "stay away from those kids."

He tied Dorjee's hands and stuffed his mouth with waste cloth, loaded him on to a Jeep and closed it with the rain cover.

Dawa stayed away from all this, he was not expecting all these theatrics to go on in his garage. He stood in a corner.

"Take Wangmo to a hospital and drop him to his place," Kanhaiya instructed Dawa.

Kanhaiya took Dorjee to a secret place behind the ashram and tied him to a chair and told the Army sepoys to take care of him and returned to the ashram.

When Kanha entered the room, Vivaant and Sukheshni were chatting after having their evening coffee in the pleasant weather.

Kanha greeted them and asked, "Your way back should be arranged in a few days. But I think you are enjoying more at Guruji's sessions, am I right Vivaant?"

"Yes, I am enjoying these sessions. Guruji is knowledgeable. It's my fortune that I was able to join these sessions," Vivaant said gratefully.

Kanhaiya and the other volunteers at the dining hall joined Vivaant and Sukheshni in serving the dishes. After dinner they went out on their usual walk before retiring for the night.

The next day morning even before Vivaant was awake, Kanhaiya went to his secret place where he had imprisoned Dorjee and started pressurizing him to know about the secrets of the Dhithi Research Labs and what they wanted.

Dorjee was a tough nut to crack and it would not be easy to make words come out of his mouth. He was a loyal servant of Mr Tarak.

Kanhaiya told his men to give special treatment to Dorjee so that he would open his mouth and returned to the ashram.

Vivaant and Sukheshni woke up and got ready for the yoga sessions. When Kanhaiya returned, Vivaant asked, "Where had you been?"

Kanhaiya said, "Nowhere, I was out on some work. There is good news, your transport to Lucknow has been arranged and you guys can leave tomorrow for the check post where Colonel Veerprathap Singh has sent officers who will receive you and take you back to Sirkha camp and Lucknow from there."

Vivaant and Sukheshni were relieved but still scared to go out by knowing the importance of the pendant and the bracelet they wore. Kanhaiya asked them to handover pendant and the bracelet to Colonel Veerprathap Singh.

The second day of the session was starting in a while. All of them gathered at the hall.

Guruji greeted everyone in the hall on the second day of the speech. Everybody chanted OM following Guruji.

Guruji started speaking by smiling at Vivaant and said, "Yesterday we left here with an open question from Vivaant.

How do we know that everything faces extinction once in 25,920 years? I had explained yesterday that the Sun and Sirius revolve around each other in a binary star system.

Each star crosses the other's orbit in one cycle of 25,920 years. When they come closer to each other; as the

Sun is smaller than Sirius, they both have their magnetic fields.

We know that even our Earth has a magnetic field and it behaves like a bar magnet with magnetic poles at the north and south. What would happen if such a strong magnet revolves around in a half-circle around a smaller magnet? The magnet rotates, and the shift in polarity happens across the Solar System.

This causes a complete shift in polarity on Earth which in turn causes tsunamis, earthquakes, volcanoes, etc. These disasters destroyed major settlements of men and women on Earth. Earth's landmass has a short life span.

The more intelligent species like reptilians and ocean beings alone can survive such tragedies. They had known these disasters would happen and had built underground cities which are much safer."

Vivaant raised his hands when Guruji signaled and allowed him to speak. "But how are human species surviving such cataclysms or such mass destruction?" Vivaant asked.

"Sadly, we don't!" replied Guruji.

"Each of these cycles is called one Manvantara or one cycle of Manu. We are living in the seventh Manvantara. There are six Manvantaras or six generations of humans have lived on Earth before us. Even scientists say the same thing. You can check on Google that homo sapiens appeared and started spreading all over the Earth 1,70,000 years ago. Both dates match perfectly - 25,920 multiplied by six generations are 1,55,000 years and 16,000 years of this Manvantara is 1,70,000 years.

There are many species of a generation of humans on this Earth that are extinct. Those species had varying capacities of human intelligence, physique, and strength.

Some research says humans of previous generations were taller and their sensory organs were much advanced and there were giants in some generations. And everyone one of those generations is extinct."

Guruji saw everyone's face and most of them looked worried.

Guruji smiled and continued, "The only way we can survive is our God should save us, shouldn't he?

The only way we humans can be saved is we have to go to a safe location till the destruction is over and everything is settled down with its new magnetic north and south poles intact."

Everyone nodded. "Then don't worry, our Gods will come and take us to such a safe place on their loka. The first Manvantara was 1,70,000 years ago.

Swarga Loka is located in the Sirius star system. Swarga Loka is a planet with exceptional technologies and advanced civilization is prevalent over the Swarga Loka which can save humans and help them evolve with their advanced technologies.

Not only Bhuloka, but there is another planet in our Solar System which is Bhuvarloka that hosts life which is our neighbouring planet in this Solar System.

This is one of the main reasons for our remarkable advancements in Satyayuga as Swargaloka is near to us. So, we can easily travel there and share their technologies.

Our Earth's most ancient findings of advanced civilizations were from Satyayuga.

Devas in Swargaloka will help us evolve into new intelligent beings and will help us to come and settle in Bhuloka and Bhuvarloka which are in the habitable zone of the Solar System.

Mars also had an atmosphere which was destroyed several millenniums ago. Not only humans, but most of the animal species evolved on Swargaloka.

So, we do not need to worry as our gods will save us. Mahavishnu will be with us in all our difficult times to save our lives at the end of the sixth Manvantara. Gods came and saved most of the animals and many species were evolved on Swargaloka and some species were resent to Bhuloka and some were sent to Bhuvarloka in the seventh Manvantara in which we are living now." Guruji concluded his speech by looking at the confused faces in the gathering.

Everyone were in awe with mouths open to form a perfect 'O' rewinding the idea implanted by Guruji.

Guruji spoke on the other question which Vivaant raised, "Yes, these calendars and numbers which we refer today are based on Before Christ and Anno Domini and Hindu calendars also are referenced with some kings as Shalivahana, etc.

But will these be referenced as the same in another 5,000 years because this calendar was not there before 2000 years?

Our calendars were once written based on astronomical calculations and our references to zodiac calculations are valid for all the 12 constellations, i.e., 25,920 years of the calendar at the time of Ramayana and Mahabharata.

Each day can easily be referred to the zodiac constellation and the location of the star and planets.

That is the reason why Indian Institute of Research on Vedas could trace back dates of the Ramayana and the Mahabharata as they were written in that manner. And our Kundalis are written in such a way we all wonder if astrology means something.

I will ask one thing to my young generation - do you believe in predictions made by your Artificial Intelligence algorithms?"

Sukheshni said, "Yes, those are designed with so much data and predictions are based on historical data."

Guruji said, "You are correct my child, why don't you guys think that astrology is written based on such data from millions of people based on their kundalis as to how they lived and for which astronomical dates which planetary position played what role in their lives. But it was done thousands of years ago.

Only a few people have proper knowledge of it and most of it is interpreted wrongly as planets which play a major role in our lives are blamed for our bad luck and poojas are performed in trying to avoid it.

There are always two faces of what you see; you should be aware of what you believe is true.

I wish to finish my speech. If anybody has any questions let us discuss or else after lunch, we shall have meditation." As no one had questions they left for lunch.

Chapter 3

PRELUDE OF A NEW MAHAYUGA

12000 BC

Swargaloka

Indra, the King and ruler of Swarga Loka had invited all the great sages and Maharishis from Maharloka to discuss on the new generation of Manavas and Danavas being safely sent to Bhuloka and Bhuvarloka respectively.

Indra wanted the Maharishis to lead them on their journey and help them and their many generations to gain knowledge and to grow spiritually and technologically.

Indra entered the Sabha hall and greeted all the Maharishis with a namaskar.

"We have assembled here for the seventh time to discuss on the seventh Manvantara. The last six Manvantaras were successful in rehabilitating the Earth with newer generations of humans stronger and capable and it had been our gift, so that we could save many species of Bhuloka and Bhuvarloka when the Solar System is going through its polar shift phase.

It has given us a unique opportunity every time that we could help Manavas and Danavas to evolve into a more knowledgeable and stronger next generation.

Many Rishis headed by Kashyapa Brahma have been able to evolve the new generation of Manavas, Danavas, and humanoids like Vanaras, Varahas, Narasimhas, Garudas, etc., into more advanced intelligent and stronger species." Indra addressed the gathering.

"I Invite Kashyapa Brahmaji to spread light on the new generation of species," Indra welcomed Kashyapa.

Kashyapa Brahma took the stage and everyone stood up and greeted him with a namaskar. Kashyapa was dark complexioned, well-built and was always seen wearing a dhoti and angavastram. With pitch black long hair tied up in a knot on the head, his long beard covered the neck. He called his wives, Aditi and Dhithi to join him on the stage. He greeted all the Maharishis with a namaskar and gestured Aditi to go on.

"The evolved generations of Manavas, the descendants of the last Manu who carry forward their generations have the same traits but are now far more knowledgeable beings than previous Manvantaras.

I believe they should be able to live peacefully on the planet along with other humanoid species and will not disturb the ecosystem of the planet and should be able to build marvellous cities on Earth and make state-of-the-art scientific advancements in future." Aditi addressed the gathering by explaining about Manavas.

Kashyapa Brahmaji said, "Aditiji and I have closely been observing this generation of Manavas. They are deeply spiritual beings and intelligent. They are devoted towards Mahavishnu and will emerge as prominent species of life on the Earth.

I believe that the Nagas and Matsyas can coexist on Earth with other humanoid species like Varahas, Vanaras, Narasimhas, Garudas, etc. Other species on the Earth can help Manavas. The technical knowledge of Manavas will help Bhuloka to achieve a new peak in its technological advancements."

Kashyapa invited Dhithiji to speak about Danavas.

"Danavas are now evolved as a much stronger and tougher species and need to survive somewhat harsher conditions of Bhuvarloka than the previous generation. They will successfully be able to achieve anything they desire because of their physical nature.

They need good guidance from a great Rishi and they can be the greatest rulers the world has ever seen. They have lengthier life span as compared to Manavas.

With their superior strength, they can build many architectural marvels. But they should not fall into the wrong hands. So, I request a great guru to lead them on the right path." Dhithi addressed the gathering by explaining about the Danavas.

Kashyapa said, "Now it's in the hands of the Maharishis to lead the Manavas and Danavas on their path towards growth."

Looking at the Maharishis Indra spoke, "As Kashyapa Brahmaji said we need Maharishis to help them in achieving great feats.

Now I will leave the decision to Maharishi Brighu and I know he will need some time to think about it. By that time, I request you Maharishis to accept our hospitality."

Maharloka

Shukracharya was young and brilliant; there was no match to his caliber in the Shastras. Angirasa had taught him more than he had to anyone, because Shukra could grasp anything that Angirasa taught.

Shukra was wheat complexioned and was shorter than his father. Angirasa had observed a specific behavior of Shukra which made him worry at times. Shukra was cunning, he could turn anyone or any situation in his favour and could go to any extent to accomplish it.

He had many dreams and wanted to scale great heights, he heard from his father about the resources available on Bhuloka and how he could use them to create modern weapons and train kings of Manukula to conquer Swargaloka and one fine day he could take his revenge.

He knew his father would want to go, so there was a chance he could accompany him. Shukracharya hated Indra for a reason. Shukra and Brihaspati were studying in Maharloka under Maharishi Angirasa.

Both were intelligent but Shukra was far more capable than Brihaspati and they knew one day one of them would be sent to become a high priest at Swargaloka.

Shukra was talented and gifted like his father, Brighu. The day came when Indra came to Maharloka to appoint a high priest to Swargaloka.

Indra needed some favour from Angirasa Maharishi. So, Indra thought that if he appointed his son Brihaspati as high priest that would please Angirasa and he would take his side when he needed a favour and he chose Brihaspati even after seeing the capability of Shukra.

Angirasa knew Shukra would not be happy. But the decision was not in his hands to make.

"Child, I know you are a gifted Rishi and one day you will reach the zenith of your greatness. Don't let this anger turn negative; always channel it positively." Angirasa counseled Shukra.

Shukra thought that Indra and Angirasa must have played politics and that image had been deeply buried in his mind.

Shukra was waiting for the day he could take revenge on Indra. Finally, the day was approaching. Indra had appointed his father Maharishi Brighu to select the team that would lead the Manavas and Danavas to Bhuloka and Bhuvarloka.

Swargaloka

After some time, all the Maharishis assembled at the Sabha Hall.

Maharishi Brighu addressed the gathering and greeted everyone and said, "This is a great responsibility that has been laid upon us by seeking the blessing of Brahmaji.

We had this discussion a few days ago with Brahmaji and decided that a team of Saptharishis will accompany the Manavas and Danavas.

These Saptharishis will be flagbearers for seven different types of knowledge transfer that is needed for both Manavas and Danavas.

So, I Brighu, with a team of Saptharishis will travel to Bhuloka with the Manavas and King Manu and will provide knowledge for the Manavas throughout their journey.

And with my pride, I will appoint Shukra with great faith in him to lead the Saptharishis to transfer knowledge similarly to the Danavas on Bhuvarloka."

Shukra did not know how to respond - to be happy that his father had such great faith that he made him the leader of Saptharishis and was leading Danavas or be sad that he did not get to go to Bhuloka and be part of the team his father had chosen, and he knew all the great Maharishis would accompany his father.

In a way, Shukra was happy as he had to lead the strongest of the lot, who were poised to become the greatest rulers of the world. If he trained them well with the technological knowledge he had, he could easily overthrow Indra one day.

Brighu with his team of Saptharishis instructed them to look after the Manavas under the leadership of King Manu and train them to leave for Bhuloka in a few days.

Shukra also went with his team to train the Danavas who were under the leadership of the brothers, the strongest of the Danavas - Hiranyakashipu and Hiranyaksha. Shukra felt happy by seeing the strength of the Danavas and prepared them for the journey to Bhuvarloka.

Chapter 4

VIVAANT'S FATHER

After guru's session, everyone was wondering about the idea of how they came into existence. Later, in the evening Kanha instructed Vivaant and Sukheshni to get prepared, as they had to leave tomorrow, and he had spoken to Colonel Veerprathap Singh on their safe travel.

Kanha left the ashram telling Vivaant and Sukheshni that he had some work.

Vivaant was curious as always about Kanhaiya's work. So, he followed him without getting noticed. There was a path behind the ashram leading to a small room where two army men were guarding it.

They saluted Kanhaiya when he went inside. Vivaant looked from a distance. He came to know that it was some secret place where Kanhaiya was working on his operations on Dhithi Research Labs. Vivaant went behind the small room near a window.

Vivaant saw someone was tied to a chair and was already beaten up badly. Kanha took a chair and spoke.

"Dorjee, I neither need you nor your life. It isn't precious to me or to your boss. You know, even if I leave you now, your boss will kill you thinking you might have leaked the information. So, you should co-operate with us rather than getting beaten up and simply waste your life and my bullets.

If you co-operate, I will promise you a safe passage out of Tibet to a place of your choice. I know you have been a loyal servant of your master all these years. Tell me whatever you know and let's be done with it."

Dorjee spoke through his bloody mouth, "How can I be sure, I will be spared and will be safely moved? I need to speak with someone I know."

Kanha smiled and replied, "Don't think I am a fool to let you speak to someone so that they can track me. You don't have any choice now than to trust my words or die. I think this is the best possible option you have, take it or leave it."

Vivaant who was hearing all of this from outside the window was curious about what Dorjee would say. Dorjee started reacting to the offer which Kanha proposed.

"Ok, that is all I know. I have rarely met Mr Tarak but I work with Devaant Sir. They have imprisoned an old man from the last twenty years it seems.

A few months ago they have been able to somehow get the treasure box which was hidden somewhere near Mt Kailash.

We were given the task to find it and bring it to him. We thought there would be lots of gold and diamonds but surprisingly it was not heavy, and it was locked in some strange ancient manner and we were unable to open it.

We thought of breaking it but Devaant Sir had clear instructions that it should be opened carefully after much research. We found it needs some kinds of keys which were small and needs to be inserted in the openings which the box had and then alone it would open.

Mr Tarak somehow got to know about the keys from the old man. Tarak Sir has an uncanny ability to make people talk without any strain.

We were then instructed to get the pendant and the bracelet from those kids. I guess those are the keys. We insisted that we would take the keys when they were in Bangalore.

Mr Tarak told us not to take any risk outside and not to create any scene where we do not have much support and wanted to finish off these kids here in Tibet.

Maybe he never wanted anyone to even know about the keys," Dorjee blabbered everything he knew.

Vivaant stood startled upon hearing the news. But he was happy to hear the news that an old man captured twenty years ago was still alive and there was every possibility that it was his kidnapped father. Vivaant realized a hard truth that they won't let him live after the secret of the box was out.

Bang! Soldiers hit on back of Vivaant's head. The sepoys carried him inside the room.

The sepoys reported to Kanhaiya that he was listening to the conversation from behind the window.

"It's ok, I know the boy. Take the boy to the ashram and get him to rest in my room," Kanhaiya instructed the sepoys.

Kanha assured Dorjee of a safe passage after all this was over and told the sepoys to give him food and went back to his room in the ashram.

Vivaant opened his eyes in his room after a while and saw Kanha sitting in front of him.

Kanhaiya offered him a glass of water and said, "I don't care what you heard but if it was someone else other than you, they would have been dead by now. I don't know what you were thinking when you followed me and came there and what you are thinking now but this is far more dangerous than you can imagine.

You can lose your life and if you stay here for a few days the result will be unthinkable. Those guys are serious; I have observed them over the years.

Mr Tarak has high connections and he can finish off you guys and we cannot do anything because this is not even our turf to play on.

As much as I have heard from Dorjee, Tarak poses a serious threat to you and Sukheshni's life.

Even if the Chinese Government gets a clue that we have a secret military post and work here they will be ready to wage war with that single reason.

In the nation's interest and your safety, it's better you leave this evening. I have made all the arrangements and please hand over the pendant and bracelet to Colonel Veerprathap Singh."

Kanha saw all the happiness in Vivaant's eyes fading away. Someone knocked on the door. When Kanha opened the door, Sukheshni entered the room. She saw Vivaant had some injury on his head and asked what happened. Both Vivaant and Kanha replied together, "Nothing."

"So, you are all packed and ready? You both should leave the ashram by evening," Kanha smiled and asked Sukheshni.

Vivaant spoke in a stubborn voice "I am not going anywhere."

Sukheshni gave a shocked look at Vivaant unaware of the happenings but Kanha maintained his cool and looked at Vivaant, "Look, I don't want you guys to get into any trouble. This is dangerous."

Sukheshni looked serious and asked, "Guys, what's this about?"

"But he might be my dad!" Vivaant looked at Kanha and spoke. Sukheshni looked shocked.

Vivaant continued, "After two decades I have got a chance to see him and talk to him. I need to save him.

I have seen my mom for 20 years every day waiting for him to return and talk to her. I want to take him to my mom and this is the responsibility of a son.

If Tarak somehow opens the box, he won't let my father live. He is alive because the box isn't opened yet."

Sukheshni still looked shocked to hear all of this and she didn't know what she missed and where was this all coming from. She could not control her curiosity and asked Vivaant, "How do you know your dad is alive?"

"I heard from Kanha's captive killer who was behind us. They work for Mr Tarak, our sponsor, the head of Dhithi Group of companies.

He brought us here so he could finish us off and get the pendant and the bracelet to open a secret treasure box and after that, he will kill my father," explained Vivaant.

"He is the murderer of my father; I want my revenge too." She turned towards Kanha and stubbornly said, "I am not going anywhere either."

"Look guys this is not about me or you. By now Tarak would have found out someone is saving you from Wangmo. He has high contacts.

I have clear instructions to close this operation and shut this down. The Chinese army is on high alert now. If Tarak gets a clue, he will come after us and destroy us. He can easily inform the Chinese Government and pose us as a threat to the Chinese military from the Indian Government." Kanha tried to convince them.

"Okay fine. You can close this operation. I will go alone and get my father back from the clutches of Tarak. I don't need anyone else." Vivaant argued with Kanha.

"This is not about you. This is a serious threat to the nation's security. If they find out that the Ashram sheltered you, the whole Ashram shall be in danger," Kanha argued.

"Tarak needs us, our pendant and bracelet. That's why he sponsored us. He won't even think of informing the Chinese Government and tell them to capture us. He won't risk the secret treasure. Till he opens it, he won't try anything risky." Sukheshni added to the heated discussion.

"That's correct. We have an advantage as long as we have the keys with us. Let us attack him first and surprise him. We should not give him time to think. Please, Kanha help us and tell me where my dad is being kept captive," Vivaant tried to convince Kanha.

Kanha knew Vivaant wouldn't stop. After all, it was his father, no one would have stopped. Kanha sighed and looked at them.

"I am shutting down this operation today officially. I can't let you both handle this alone. It poses a serious threat to the nation. The only person who may help us after hearing this story is Colonel Veerprathap Singh.

I will be there with you guys. But first, we have to plan on how to handle this situation. You guys take rest. I will speak to the Colonel and return in a while." Kanha said looking at them.

Dhithi Research Labs

Tarak's boys had finally found the person who had tackled Wangmo and Dorjee was an Indian officer.

Mr Tarak used all his influence politically to stop Kanhaiya. He knew that he could cross any of his limits to save those kids.

He had pressurized the Indian Government to close all their RAW operations on Tibetan soil. Following that, the Indian Government had issued a notice to Kanhaiya to shut down all his operations.

Sitting in his office, Mr Tarak curled up his lips and told Devaant, "I don't think any officer will come between us and those kids who are hiding in the ashram. Go and get their pendant and bracelet and finish them off. Time has finally come to see what is being hidden in the box from centuries."

Ashram

"It's not safe to be in the ashram, at any time Tarak can send his boys to get you guys. Let's move everything to a safer place.

A few kilometers inside the forest there is a safe hideout where we can stay and get food supplies from the ashram by one of our close aides.

We will inform the ashram that we have left for India and will make arrangements such that one of the military checkpoints repeats the same. For that, we have to send you passports with some people to make proper entries and make sure it is recorded at entry and exit checkpoints." Kanhaiya instructed Vivaant and Sukheshni to quickly make arrangements and had a telephonic conversation with the Colonel.

Kanhaiya explained the plan to the Colonel, "Sir, please arrange two people who resemble Vivaant and Sukheshni so that they can be sent back to India with Vivaant and Sukheshni's passports out of the Chinese border.

The Colonel was not happy about the plan of risking those kids' lives but he understood and respected their emotions and had belief in Kanhaiya and was sure he wouldn't let anything happen to them.

Devaant sent a few of his people to bring Vivaant and Sukheshni from the ashram. But by the time they reached they got to know Vivaant and Sukheshni had vacated early morning to proceed to India. They knew they couldn't apprehend them once they passed the border. They went in search of them but could not find them.

Kanhaiya gave the passports to Vivaant and Sukheshni's impersonates. They had the same hairstyle and physique; both were from the army as Vivaant and Sukheshni were athletes they had a well-built physique like army men and women. They took their clothes and bag and went to the check-post to get a pass to India.

Wangmo and the others were stationed close to the checkpoint. Wangmo recognized their bags and clothes but they could not do anything to go near them.

They informed Devaant about the same. He told them it was okay and he would send someone to get the pendant and the bracelet once they were in India.

Chapter 5

SHUKRA'S PLAN

Swargaloka

Shukra had one obstacle to his plan to take revenge on Indra. He feared only one man in the world and that was Brighu, his father.

He knew it would be impossible for him to proceed to execute any of his plans until and unless his father was around. He knew he could handle all the Saptharishis but not his father. He thought of a plan to send him back to Maharloka.

When all the Rishis had assembled, Shukra spoke, "Father I am delighted you have chosen me to lead the Danavas. But my only worry is who will train these Rishis to become great Rishis like the Saptharishis in all areas of knowledge.

Who will guide them to become a great Maharishi? I think such a great teacher like Maharishi Brighu should not be limited to Bhuloka, but he should be available to all the lokas and welfare of all the fourteen worlds."

For the first time, all the Devas and Rishis including Devaraja Indra nodded to the wise words of Shukra but no one knew his intent. None of them would have dreamt of what Shukra had on his mind. Indra had also feared Brighu Maharishi. He thought if Brighu was not there he could easily bring Bhuloka and Bhuvarloka under his control.

Maharishi Brighu also agreed it would be wise of him to stay in Maharloka and prepare other Rishis and have full confidence in his son and other rishis.

Everyone prayed to Brahma and Mahavishnu to come and bless the Manavas and Danavas and help them reach Bhuloka and Bhuvarloka.

Brahma and Mahavishnu blessed everyone.

Shukra knew if he could get the Pushpaka Vimana from Brahma it would be an easier journey.

"O Great Brahma, the creator of this Universe, bless us and show us the path to Bhuvar Loka," Shukra prayed to Brahma.

Brahma gave his Pushpaka Vimana built by Vishwakarma to Shukra. "It can take you anywhere in the Solar System within a short time and can land anywhere you need it and instructed him to take the Danavas to Bhuvarloka." Brahma blessed Shukra.

Shukra obliged Brahma and took Hiranyakashipu and Hiranyaksha and the other Danavas to Bhuvarloka.

"O Mahavishnu and great Brahma bless us and show us the path to Bhuloka," the Saptharishis prayed to Brahma and Vishnu.

The Saptharishis revealed their worry, "The Earth has three-fourths of its surface covered with water. It will be difficult for us Rishis also to use our normal Vimana to land on Bhuloka's land surface. This is the time after the pralaya has taken place and the oceans will be harsh."

The Vimana did not have technological advancements as Pushpaka Vimana which could easily hover over the land till the rider found a safe place to land on.

"Saptharishis don't worry, believe me everything will go fine. You will get help from Matsyas once you land on the Ocean," Vishnu blessed the Saptharishis and Manu.

The Saptharishis along with the Manavas and Shukra's team with Danavas left Swargaloka for their respective planets.

Saptharishis and Manu took their Vimana and came towards Bhuloka. After a few years of travel, the Vimana crashed and landed in the Arabian Sea. The Oceans were violent, it was difficult to hold the Vimana in the ocean. The Oceans were not welcoming. The Vimana was rolling and tumbling due to the Ocean's currents.

Matsyaraja Matsyendra was a half-human half-aquatic Merman. He was the King and ruler of the seven oceans and was fair-complexioned with long hair and having half body of a giant fish in blue colour. He had seen all the six Manvantaras flourish and vanish in front of his eyes. He knew it was part of a cycle of life and death. It was always a Matsyaraja's responsibility to help the start of a new manvantara by helping land beings with their needs.

Matsyendra knew it was time when the Saptharishis arrived on Bhuloka. He had ordered all the kingdoms of the seven oceans to let him know the arrival of Saptharishis.

Matsyendra got information that a Vimana had crash landed on the Indian ocean. Matsyaraja went with his team and saved the Saptharishis and Manu.

The Saptharishis and Manu thanked him and bowed to him. The Saptharishis blessed him and his kingdom to flourish in the times to come.

Matsyendra said, "It's my pleasure that I will be helpful towards your cause. We have an advanced submarine which will take you to land safely."

"The Manavas will always be indebted for your help. You are a form of Mahavishnu to us to help and save Manavas to flourish on Bhuloka." Manu took blessings from Matsyendra.

The Manavas and Saptharishis took the submarine and travelled towards Jambudwipa.

Note: The Sumerian Texts also say that a fish-man Oannes brought behind seven seers and guided them during the great deluge, the same as in Matsyapurana of Hindu literature.

After a few years of his rule, Manu realized by seeing the whole land of Jambudwipa that there was no wealth and needs of Manukula were many. Manu prayed to Mahavishnu to make him capable of satisfying all the needs of Manukula.

Mahavishnu appeared before him, "Manu, all that the Manavas need is present on this Bhuloka. You need not search anywhere."

Manu persisted in his opinion, "But there is no wealth and richness as I had heard or dreamt of on Bhuloka."

"Wealth and richness are not a way to seek fulfilment but if you persist, all that you need is available on Bhuloka on Mandara Parvata which is submerged in the ocean now.

You pray to Kurmaraja and take the help of Kurmas who will search for Mandara Parvata in the underground and will get whatever you need to satisfy Manukula," Vishnu blessed Manu.

Manu prayed to Kurmaraja to help him to bring wealth and make him capable of satisfying the needs of Manukula.

Kurmaraja was as old as the oceans itself. He was wise and detached from all the worldly pleasures and wealth. He lived in isolation from the whole world in an underground city called Mandaravati under Mandara Parvata. But he always helped whoever was in need.

Kurmaraja came and asked, "Manu, with all this wealth will you be able to satisfy all the needs of Manavas? I have seen many generations of Manavas on this Bhuloka and I know this will not help."

"Yes, I would and want to satisfy the needs of Manavas. Please help me in bringing the wealth submerged under the ocean to the land," Manu requested Kurmaraja.

Kurmaraja said, "Wealth does not bring happiness and prosperity; the happiness is only for that moment. I know what will help Manukula to flourish on this beautiful Bhuloka of ours."

Kurmaraja went inside the ocean and brought all the Ratnas, the wealth needed for Manukula and he said that this wealth would help Manu to establish his kingdom in all the riches and would help him lead his kingdom towards a prosperous future.

Kurmaraja brought and blessed Manu with the Kalpavriksha and said that he would get whatever he prayed for with this Kalpavriksha from Mandaravati.

Kurmaraja gifted the Kamadhenu which would help Manu to plough the land and start a civilization on the banks of river Saraswati.

"This is mother Kamadhenu which has helped many generations of Manavas to flourish on Bhuloka. Kamadhenu with other cows of its kind will help nomads and hunter-gatherers to settle down and start a family. This will help Manavas to start a new way of life.

Kamadhenu will give milk for humans wherever they settle, its dung will be a good fertilizer for the land and its urine can be used as an antibiotic for their diseases," Kurmaraja said.

Manu was blessed to hear all of this and thanked Kurmaraja and told him, "Humans will forever be indebted to you and will worship you my lord."

Kamadhenu helped the Manavas to settle down and start a civilized life on the banks of river Saraswati. The Manavas worshipped Kamadhenu as a goddess.

Manu with the help of wealth, Kalpavriksha and Kamadhenu led the new civilization and helped his fellow Manavas to lead a prosperous and orderly life.

As years flew by, the desires of Manavas grew. Desires turned into greed. Greed turned their life from happy to miserable. Manu was fed up of resolving the issues and satisfying every one of his people.

Manu again prayed to Mahavishnu after a few years. When Mahavishnu appeared before Manu, "Even after trying so much and in spite of having everything I cannot fulfil all the desires of the Manavas. What should I do?

Please advise me on how to satisfy all the desires of the Manavas," asked Manu.

Mahavishnu smiled and replied, "But when Kurmaraja asked, will you be able to satisfy all the needs; you had said, yes."

Manu bowed his head and apologized. "I am as ignorant as a child my lord, forgive me. I am a fool who thought wealth can satisfy the desires of Manavas."

"Instead of doing *Manthana* of the ocean and finding all the wealth, Manavas should do *Manthana* of their own *Manas* to find the answers and realize that they already have what they need. Desires are never ending. It does not mean desires are bad. Desire drives humans to achieve great things. If it turns to greed, it will spoil everything.

Swamanthana is the most important thing to do for self-realization on how Manavas should consciously react to their desires. To achieve what they need, there will always be many ways but they should consciously choose the right path even if the wrong path is short and easy. It is your responsibility to preach that to the Manavas," Mahavishnu advised Manu.

Manu bowed to Mahavishnu and realized that no wealth could put an end to the desires of the Manavas and promised Mahavishnu that he would try to preach and lead Manavas on the path to self-realization.

Secret Army Outpost

Vivaant and Sukheshni sat with Kanha and waited for news from the Colonel that their impersonates had cleared the check post and entered India. Kanha went out and attended a call from the Colonel who was happy to inform Kanha that their plan had worked.

Vivaant was eager to get out and save his father from the clutches of Tarak. The person whom he had hated his whole life was his mission now, but he had no idea of what to do or where to go to find his father.

Vivaant went towards the photo of Shri Krishna and started praying, "God, please show me the way to find my father and save him. Please help me this time, I will never ask for anything again in my life. I need to bring a smile back on my mother's face and that is the only desire I have in my life"

Vivaant looked at Kanha and said, "Kanha, you have agreed to help me. Come let's go and capture Tarak and get my father out of that hell."

Kanha said, "Asking god for help, reacting to the situation like this is the natural tendency of a human. I will tell you a story about humans and their desires and then you decide what the right thing to do is."

Kanha narrated the story of Kurmavatar and told him that they should not always seek answers from God when they have everything they know within and they would find a way and we should always react to our internal desires consciously. We should not take any short cuts.

Kanha elaborated, "Let's analyze the data we have now." Everyone started by telling whatever they knew.

Sukheshni started, "Vishwanath uncle and dad went in search of something near Mount Kailash. So, there might be some clues near Mount Kailash."

Vivaant said, "Dhithi Research Labs is obviously involved. We can track their employees and can try to get information out of them."

Kanha replied "Yes, we can track Wangmo and some of Tarak's boys about their daily routine, so that we might get some info on where they have hidden Vishwanath Sir."

"I have a very good friend of mine, a Tibetan special officer who is a part of the secret force which guards places such as Mt Kailash. His name is Lhawang.

He might be the right person to do this work and help us in finding Vishwanath Sir. It might be risky for us; as Chinese police would be verifying that I have closed my operation and have gone back to India." Kanha told Vivaant and Sukheshni.

Chapter 6

AVATARS

Manu flourished Bhuloka with greenery with the blessings of Kalpavriksha and cultivated Bharata Kanda, the land on the banks of rivers with the help of Kamadhenu. Manu helped all other species on Bhuloka to live happily.

On Bhuvarloka, Shukra got news of the glory of Bhuloka and its beauty and all the help Mahavishnu endowed on Manavas. Shukra got a feeling that the gods have chosen a side and cheated him and have not given anything to the Danavas.

Shukra filled Hiranyaksha and Hiranyakashipu with these words and they were also feeling the heat of jealousy.

Shukra guided them to get power by doing *tapasya* on Brahma so that they would become immortal and they could control Swargaloka and Bhuloka.

Hiranyaksha went to do long *tapasya* on Brahma standing on one leg for many years. Many showers of rain, thunder, burning heat of Surya and cyclones did not hinder him. As the strongest Danava, Hiranyaksha's capacity was tested to its limits and finally, he succeeded in pleasing Brahma.

Brahma appeared in front of him and said, "Son, wake up, state your wish, I have come here to fulfil it."

"Brahmaji thanks for asking me. Please bless me with the boon of immortality," asked Hiranyaksha.

"I can't give that to anyone my child. Any creation must and will eventually lead to destruction. Please ask anything other than that." Brahma told him.

Hiranyaksha thought that the only thing that could kill him was Indra's Vajrayudha, Shiva's Trishul and Vishnu's Sudarshana Chakra.

"I should not die from any Shastras or Astras in the whole universe," said Hiranyaksha.

"I, Brahma bless you that you will not meet your death by any Shastras or Astras" Brahma said.

Hiranyaksha who was delighted came back and told Hiranyakashipu in front of Shukra, "I am ready to defeat anyone in this world. Please bless me to go and conquer Bhuloka and Swargaloka and make you the King of the three worlds."

While Hiranyaksha was in deep penance on Brahma, many years passed by on Bhuloka and it became home to many plants and species of beings and most of the animals and humanoids like Vanaras, Narasimhas, Varahas, Manavas and many other species came from Swargaloka and started living peacefully on Bharath Kanda or Jambudwipa.

Note: Other continents might have been home to many other humanoid species that are denoted on wall scripts in many Egyptian pyramids.

Each species ruled some areas and many princes of many clans came to study at the Saptharishis Ashrams.

Agastya Ashram

In Bharat Khand, one of the renowned gurukuls was of Agastya Muni. He taught warfare and weaponry to princes while other Rishis in his ashram taught the remaining subjects such as Vedas, Upavedas and Vedangas.

One of Agastya muni's courageous and intelligent students was Bhudhara, a Varaha. Bhudhara was dark and tough-skinned having sharp trunks and a muscular torso with the strength of a hundred elephants in his hands.

He was strong but was a child at heart, always curious about the outside world. He would play with children and enjoyed their company. He would lend his tusks to children for them to hang on and play.

Agastya Muni and all others worshipped Mahavishnu, the protector of Bhuloka. He told them stories of Matsya and Kurma avataras and how at any point of time if any problem occurs on Bhuloka, Mahavishnu would come and save them in one or the other form.

"If Mahavishnu knows all and wants to protect our Bhuloka, won't he even stop someone first before doing any harm to Bhuloka?" asked Bhudhara.

Agastya Muni smiled and explained to him the concept of Karma. "Vatsa, how can somebody get their Karmaphala before doing their karma. Karma might be good or bad and everyone will receive what they deserve for the karma they did. Anyone who commits a crime will be punished but just because one may or may not commit the crime in future, you cannot stop somebody from doing their work.

Or else everyone will have to be prisoners at one time or the other. Everyone has the potential to commit a crime."

Bhudhara nodded with a smile and asked, "How will Mahavishnu come at the exact time and stop someone from any harm being done to Bhuloka?"

"Mahavishnu will always be with us in one or the other form. He is alive in every one of us, even in you. When the time comes, he will act," Agastya Muni answered Bhudhara's query.

Attack on Kumari Kanda

Hiranyaksha took the Pushpaka Vimana with the blessings of his brother and his guru Shukra and came to Bhuloka. He looked over the beautiful continent of Kumari Kanda. His wicked mind wanted to destroy it. He knew no death now. He had got a feeling that he had become immortal.

Seated in his Pushpaka Vimana Hiranyaksha hovered over Kumari Kanda. He took his mace and hit the floor at the centre of Kumari Kanda with enormous strength. The impact was such that it felt like a nuclear blast. The tectonic plate started shaking. There was an enormous earthquake which was never felt or experienced before. Hiranyaksha created havoc on Bhuloka by repetitively hitting the land and he sent his mace deep inside the ocean to hit the ocean floor.

Bhuloka started trembling and the ocean floor opened its mouth and started swallowing the land above. Kumari Kanda started to sink. Huge tsunamis hit Bharat Kanda and all the underground cities were shaken. No one was prepared, Kings ruling the land tried to evacuate people with Vimanas and ships, but they could only save a few.

Underground cities were shaken and the Matsyas and Nagas found out about Hiranyaksha and started attacking him. Agastya sent every one of his students to save all those in trouble and he instructed his group of brave warriors led by Bhudhara. "This is caused by something with a huge impact on Kumari Kanda, go to the seashore and pray to Vasuki, the King of Nagas. Matsyas and Nagas might be fighting, go and help them," Agastya Muni instructed Bhudhara.

Bhudhara was still waiting as to when would Mahavishnu appear and save them. He went to the seashore and prayed to Vasuki. Obliged by Bhudhara's prayers Vasuki came out of the ocean. After looking at Bhudhara he knew that he was no ordinary Varaha but was an incarnation of Vishnu.

Vasuki carried Bhudhara on top of his seven hoods and went to the middle of the ocean where Hiranyaksha was creating havoc.

Bhudhara used all his weaponry knowledge and chanted many mantras and tried to shoot him down with powerful arrows. Hiranyaksha stood there laughing wickedly at Bhudhara. Bhudhara tried to hit him with his mace and Hiranyaksha took the hits and showed the world how strong he was.

Vasuki told Bhudhara, "I have heard he has a boon from Brahma that no Astras or Shastras can kill him."

"I know, he wants to show off that he is strong, he is a fool, and he does not know he is getting weaker by tolerating these attacks," Bhudhara told Vasuki.

Bhudhara finally invited him to a duel. Hiranyaksha was strong but was weakened by earlier attacks of Bhudhara. Hiranyaksha was still able to put down Bhudhara twice. Next time when Bhudhara was pushed down, he voluntarily went down and struck at Hiranyaksha's chest with his sharp trunks. Bhudhara lifted him with his trunks and threw him off ending his life.

Vasuki with bowed hands sang Varaha stuti and made him realize his true potential of being an avatar of Mahavishnu.

Bhudhara appeared in Virata Roopa of Mahavishnu in Varaha avatar and blessed everyone.

Tsunamis calmed down along with the earthquakes but a whole continent with the Sangam culture was lost in the depths of the ocean. Thus, started the declining phase of Satyayuga by the end of Kumari Kanda.

Note: The event occurred around 10000 BC i.e., 12000 years ago, long before the Mahabharata and the Ramayana happened. There are hardly any remains of Sangam literature.

In the 18th century, a European scientist discovered the hypothetical Lemuria continent which might have been submerged in the Indian or the Pacific Ocean.

Secret Army Camp

Kanha mentioned the idea of handling the Dhithi Research Labs investigation to the Chinese special officer Lhawang.

Vivaant expressed his dislike for giving the responsibility of this case to Chinese when they could do it. Tarak could easily influence any of the Chinese Government officers and he wanted to handle it himself.

"They do not work for the Chinese Government. They are special officers who take care of mysterious places which might hold some secrets and guard them.

So, there is no need to worry. Tarak cannot influence him as you think," said Kanha.

Vivaant replied, "But, we can handle it ourselves."

Kanha replied, "No we cannot take the risk and he will know how to investigate the research and what all they have found out near Mt Kailash.

He is our only hope to get some valuable information about Tarak now, without taking any risk."

"But, what will we do?" was Vivaant's question. "We can't simply wait here hoping someone will do the work for us."

Kanha smiled, he knew it wasn't easy to convince a son who was on his feet to get his father back.

"Vivaant you have read a lot of Mythology. Then tell me why Vishnu himself did not kill Hiranyaksha but took Varaha avatar.

"That is because Hiranyaksha had a boon that he couldn't be killed by any weapon. So, he took the form of Varaha and killed him with his tusks." Vivaant said brushing up his knowledge of Mythology.

Kanha exclaimed, "Exactly! Every job needs its specialty. Everyone can't do everything. So, we have to wait till officer Lhawang gets back to us. I have some work; I'll go out, you guys take rest or plan something, but don't get caught in any trouble, it's not safe out there."

"Vivaant, don't worry, we will save uncle. I will be with you. I will complete the task for what my father gave his life for," Sukheshni tried to calm him down. She knew that her father was not there with her for 20 years and she was accustomed to his absence, but Vivaant was going through an emotional breakdown knowing his father was alive and his mother was suffering without him.

"Thanks, Sukheshni for everything; you have been a great support to me." Vivaant thanked her for being with him even though he had troubled her so much in college during the quarrels they had.

They both had a big laugh remembering their fights in college. Two quarrel mongers had become friends and more than friends, they were partners now. They understood each other's feelings about their families and supported each other.

Vivaant had much more respect for her as her father was martyred while trying to save his dad and brother.

Mars or Bhuvarloka

After hearing what happened to Hiranyaksha, Hiranyakashipu's fury surged through him and vowed revenge, "I will kill that cheat Vishnu, he killed my brother by cheating, he did not dare fight him, so he came in the form of Varaha and killed him, I will not spare him," he told Shukra.

"For that, you need to become strong, stronger than Hiranyaksha. Go and do *tapasya* of Brahma and get the boon of immortality, ask for your boon carefully, so that Vishnu can't deceive you this time," advised Shukra.

Hiranyakashipu took Shukra's blessings and went on to do penance on Brahma to get a boon to be immortal. He sat in penance for many years.

Indra tried many ways to stop him. He knew if Hiranyakashipu gets too powerful he would become a problem for him. Indra told Agni to rain fire, Varuna to rain thunderous showers, Vayu attacked with cyclones but

Hiranyakashipu tolerated everything. His pain from his brother's death and hate for Vishnu gave him strength.

Hiranyakashipu's wife Kayadu was pregnant. Once he left for penance, there was no one to look after Danava Loka.

Indra in Swargaloka was feeling powerless day-by-day after he heard what Hiranyaksha had become and thinking that Hiranyakashipu might be able to achieve immortality and overpower him.

The Danavas were trained by Shukra. He knew it wouldn't be long before the Danavas attacked Swargaloka and take it away from him.

Without Hiranyakashipu, there was no prominent leader for the Danavas. Indra saw this opportunity to attack Bhuvarloka and capture Kayadu and finish Hiranyakashipu and his family and thought that he could disturb his penance and destroy the entire Danava clan.

As Hiranyakashipu was praying to Brahma, it was Brahma's responsibility to take care of his devotee and his family. So, he sent his son Narada Muni to save Kayadu. Narada went to Bhuvar Loka.

Indra and the other devas had laid siege to Bhuvar Loka and wanted to kill Kayadu and her unborn child. But Narada went and took Kayadu and came to Bhuloka before that could happen and took her to his ashram and promised her that she would be safe there.

Hiranyakashipu was going strong in his penance. Kayadu gave birth to a male child, Narada Muni named him as Prahalada.

Prahalada grew up hearing chants and stories of Mahavishnu every second of his life. The Narayana jap had become part of his every breath.

As Narada was a great devotee of Vishnu, he used to sing about his greatness all day. Prahalada under his influence became the greatest devotee of Vishnu. Prahalada always believed in him with a pure heart. Prahalada even at such a young age had gained knowledge of all the subjects.

After the dawn of Kumari Kanda and Sangam civilization, many Manavas and humanoids prayed to the Varaha avatar of Vishnu and as per his wish Manavas, Vanaras, Varahas, Narasimhas and others spread out to all of the worlds and stayed in many places like India, Egypt, Middle Asia and Europe continents.

Years went by and Hiranyakashipu was still in penance to take revenge against Vishnu. Prahalada was becoming an ardent devotee of Mahavishnu in the ashram of Narada.

Narada's ashram was under the protection of Narasimha's kingdom. Narada knew that Indra would never dare attack a place under Narasimha's protection as he was aware of his rage which could destroy him.

King Ugralochana was the King of Narasimhas, whose capital was in present-day Egypt. Indra also feared the fiery eyes of Ugralochana, and that is the reason he didn't dare harm Kayadu or Prahalada at Narada's ashram.

Ugralochana had a son, Prince Vajranakha, who was the bravest and wisest of Narasimhas and had brought all humanoid species under one kingdom. He would not spare anyone who tried to hurt any of his subjects. No one would like to see the angry face of Vajranakha as it was terrifying.

If he opened his eyes, everyone in front of him would keep quiet. When any army attacked them, by hearing his roar, the whole battlefield would come to a standstill.

He loved his father and all the kingdoms had surrendered to him, admired him for his rule and justice and how he respected all and treated everyone equally.

Pleased with Hiranyakashipu's penance, Brahma appeared before him and said, "Son wake up, I am pleased with your penance, you may ask for any boon you want."

Hiranyakashipu requested Brahma to grant him the boon of immortality.

Brahma said, "I cannot give that boon to anyone in the world. So please ask any other wish that you may have."

Hiranyakashipu was angry as he knew even his brother did not get it and that had got him killed but he thought of an alternative plan.

"Grant me a boon that I should not die inside or outside, daytime or night, nor by any weapon or by any human or an animal, nor can I be killed in space or land," asked Hiranyakashipu.

"As you wish, I grant you the same," said Brahma.

Hiranyakashipu returned to his kingdom and came to know what had happened in his absence and what Indra had done. What he was planning to do to his wife and how Narada Muni saved them.

Hiranyakashipu went to Narada ashram on Bhuloka and was happy to find his wife Kayadu and son Prahalada safe. He thanked Narada Muni and took them to his kingdom.

Prahalada was always chanting Vishnu's name and offering prayers to Vishnu. Hiranyakashipu grew intolerant towards it.

"Stop chanting that Vishnu's name in front of me. He killed your uncle, he cheated the Danavas and always favoured Manavas. You should hate him and take revenge," Hiranyakashipu tried to make him understand.

"Father, Uncle tried to destroy Bhuloka and killed millions of Manavas. Vishnu did that to protect people who prayed for him. You also start praying. He will do good for us also," Prahalada tried to convince his father.

"Vishnu is not his god. I am his god and let him worship me and by that time I'll teach a lesson to Indra." Hiranyakashipu instructed Kayadu to put some sense into him.

He went to Swargaloka. Indra knew he was in grave danger and he had already escaped to Vaikuntha to ask Vishnu to save him, but Vishnu was not in Vaikuntha.

Hiranyakashipu laughed at the state of Indra and conquered Swarga Loka and designated himself as god of all the three worlds. He returned to his palace and was happy that he had conquered Swarga Loka and told Kayadu that he would kill Indra one day and complete his revenge.

He went to Prahalada thinking he would know his true power and treat him as god but Prahalada was praying to Mahavishnu.

Hiranyakashipu was so frustrated that he thundered, "See, I have conquered Swarga Loka and command all the Devas. I am the new god for all worlds. Your Vishnu has gone missing. I am your god from now on, the whole world worships me now."

"Father, I respect you and worship you as god because you are my father and out of love. The whole world worships you out of fear.

But the whole world worships Vishnu out of love because he protects them. So spread love to become god, not fear," answered Prahalada patiently.

Hiranyakashipu clenched his jaws and ordered the death of his son.

His sister Holika was immune to fire. So, he asked her to take him to the fire and burn him.

"Forgive him, my lord, he is a small child. He will realize once he comes of age. Please don't give him such a cruel punishment," Kayadu cried and requested Hiranyakashipu to forgive him.

Holika was overjoyed as she wanted her son to be the next king and she could now eliminate the competition to the throne.

Holika took him to a huge pyre generated by her. Prahalada started praying to Mahavishnu and sat on Holika's lap.

The fire started burning Holika and she was burned to ashes but nothing happened to Prahalada.

Hiranyakashipu had already lost his brother because of Vishnu. Now Holika too was gone, he was seething with anger.

Indra went to Satyaloka to ask Brahma for help, "Please help me regain Swargaloka, I have been kicked out of my own house and save all the gods from the wrath of Hiranyakashipu."

Brahma said, "You are getting the taste of your own medicine. Only Vishnu can put an end to Hiranyakashipu when the time comes."

Indra said, "But Vishnu is not in Vaikuntha, where can we find him?"

Brahma smiled and said, "Then he has already taken an avatar and will act when the time comes."

Hiranyakashipu went to Prahalada. "I will kill that Vishnu, tell me where he is, he has killed my brother and sister. I will make him pay for it, tell me where he is hiding?" shouted Hiranyakashipu.

Young Prahalada said, "He is everywhere, he is in my prayers, he is in you, he is in me, he is in space, he is on the land that you stand on, all lokas are him and he is in them."

Hiranyakashipu laughed savagely, "If your Vishnu is everywhere why won't he come before me or you? And yes, I remember you have grown fond of Vishnu when you were on Bhuloka. Your ashram might be a good place to start the search."

Hiranyakashipu went to Bhuloka and took Prahalada with him to the ashram of Narada. Narada was intelligent, he told Hiranyakashipu that this land was ruled by Ugralochana, he could go and ask him, he would help him to find Vishnu.

Hiranyakashipu knew no fear, he didn't have a care, he went to Ugralochana's palace and demanded, "I, the god of all the three lokas demand that you tell me where Vishnu is hiding. I will kill him."

Ugralochana was old and wise; he responded to Hiranyakashipu with a smile, "If you are god then you should know where god exists. He exists in the heart of every being. He is omnipresent and one who has to introduce himself as god is no god."

Hiranyakashipu was aggravated on listening to the pep talk he received. He decided to pierce Ugralochana's heart to see Vishnu.

Hiranyakashipu threw his dagger towards Ugralochana who was sitting on his throne and killed him. He then began killing everyone who attacked him and went in search of Vishnu on Bhuloka.

Hearing this news, Vajranakha reached the palace and walked slowly with wet eyes towards his father's body. He took an oath of revenge to eliminate Hiranyakashipu.

Vajranakha could not stop his growing rage; he was furious. He went alone to fight with Hiranyakashipu. All the three lokas were shaken by the rage of Vajranakha; he went into head-on battle with Hiranyakashipu.

Vajranakha and Hiranyakashipu battled with their maces. The sounds of maces colliding created tremors in all the three lokas. Vajranakha roared and kicked Hiranyakashipu on his chest till he fell to the ground.

All the devas were witnessing the whole thing. It was an intense fight. Hiranyakashipu knew he could not die at any cost because of his boon from Brahma. He had become invincible.

Vajranakha knew about Hiranyakashipu's boon and if anyone had a chance of killing him, that was him as he was neither a man nor an animal; his nails were like Indra's vajra; thus, he was called Vajranakha.

He battled him till it was twilight when it was neither day nor night. Vajranakha pulled Hiranyakashipu holding him by his hairs at the entrance of the palace, where it was neither inside nor outside at twilight, he pulled him and put him on his lap and pierced his stomach with his nails and tore him apart; thus, ending his story.

Vajranakha was on a rampage and his pain of losing his father had made him a mad hungry lion. He was destroying everything coming in his way. If he could not be controlled, everyone in the world would be in danger, no one had seen the rage of Vishnu till date.

Everyone prayed to Shiva and approached him to save Bhuloka, else Narasimha would destroy all of it. Shiva knew for any action to stop it; there must be an equal and opposite reaction.

Shiva took Sharaba avatar, a human's face with a lion's body and came to the Earth and went on head-to-head with Vajranakha. Sharaba pounced on Vajranakha, he held his hands and pushed him backwards. Vajranakha attacked him. Their battle went on for days, both had scratched each other's bodies but weren't tired.

Sharaba told Prahalada to chant a Narasimha stuti to please Vajranakha reminding him that he was Vishnu and after Prahalada chanted, Vajranakha calmed down.

In memory of Sharaba saving Bhuloka, people of Egypt built a huge structure of Sharaba on both Bhuloka and Bhuvarloka.

Note: Sphinx is a huge structure in Egypt. The exact dating is still not clear. The rain erosions show it dates much before 5000-6000 BC as it was the last when Egypt saw rain. Sphinx depicts a lion's body with human head and the oldest mention of Sphinx in history is at Gobekle Tepe in Turkey around 9500 BC.

Sharaba is also a Sphinx. He is depicted at many Hindu temples as an avatar of Shiva stopping Narasimha. Greek sphinxes are usually depicted with wings. Sharaba is depicted as a half lion and half-human with wings and lion face in some temples.

9585 BC marks the end of Satyayuga as per our cycle of Yugas.

Chapter 7

SECRETS ARE OUT

Army camp

Kanha returned to the camp after discussing with the Tibetan officer Lhawang. "I have a great piece of news. Officer Lhawang has got a blueprint of the building where they might have kept the secret box and maybe Dr Vishwanath in captivity.

I will meet him tomorrow and get it. Later, let's plan how to get the box and save him." Kanha told Vivaant and Sukheshni.

Kanha collected the blueprint of the old warehouse which had a secret underground base where Tarak had been doing all his secret work.

Kanha, Vivaant and Sukheshni sat down for a plan to go to the warehouse and studied the map where all the security guards were stationed and on ways to tackle them. They had to handle CCTVs, infrared signals and all the guards.

Kanha got the weapons ready; guns which could shoot some strong sedatives to knock out guards; he felt they were enough to finish their job.

Kanha decided on a plan and shared it with them. He gave a sedative gun to Vivaant and said, "Let us go inside; we will be connected with these earphones. Sukheshni shall guide us from the CCTV room, once we take control of it. Sukheshni will signal us in case of approaching danger. We both shall go inside and get the secret box and save Dr Vishwanath. Let us not deviate from the plan and put others' lives in danger and the last advice from me is, avoid getting killed," instructed Kanha.

"The whole thing should be executed at night though the temperature wouldn't help much. It will be freezing cold and Kanha knew Vivaant and Sukheshni wouldn't be acclimatized to that condition." They wore clothes given by Kanha which had cool gadgets integrated within.

All three of them went near the warehouse in the freezing cold with their teeth chattering. Harsh cold winds blew on their faces, Vivaant and Sukheshni were feeling suffocated, they could not breathe in the freezing cold.

Kanha told them to pull the red tag of their suits. It got heated up quickly and they felt comfortable. Kanha had a small oxygen supplier kit. Both breathed oxygen and felt a bit more relaxed now and they were ready for action.

Kanha knew he had to finish it quickly. From a far distance, they saw two security guards sitting at either end of the gates of the big warehouse. Kanha shot sedatives at the necks of both the security guards from a considerable distance.

Vivaant and Kanha moved closer towards the gate not being visible to CCTV. The guards in the CCTV room came to see what happened and why both the guards at the gate had fallen asleep.

Kanha and Vivaant slowly came behind them and shot sedatives. They sneaked into the gates and slowly closed it before anyone could notice.

Sukheshni took control of the CCTV room which was behind the gate as both guards were knocked out by Kanha and Vivaant. All the three of them saw the kind of security they had from the CCTV footage. They knew they were no match for them.

As they saw in the basement, there was a high level of security. There was a lift which directly went to the basement, but they noticed two men guarding it.

Sukheshni stayed at the CCTV room to guide them. Kanha took the lift to the basement. When the lift opened in the basement, the guards saw there was no one inside the lift.

The guards entered the lift and thought they would go and check who operated it on the upper floor. As soon as they entered and closed the door, Kanha who was hiding at the ceiling of the lift with the help of his magnetic suit injected sedatives into both of them. As soon as the lift opened, Kanha pushed the guards towards Vivaant, who was waiting outside. They pulled the guards to a side; took their IDs and weapons and went to the basement.

There was no one in the straight hallway; someone from afar shouted, "Is everything okay?" in Chinese.

"Everything is okay," Kanha replied in the same language. Vivaant who didn't have any idea of what they were talking just followed Kanha.

According to the blueprint, there was a small office portion where Tarak used to sit. The place where the box might have been hidden and the place where the captive was kept was still unknown to them.

Kanha and Vivaant moved towards Tarak's room. The guards in front of Tarak's room didn't know that these two were not guards. Kanha and Vivaant were disguised and had covered their faces with masks.

Kanha and Vivaant came near them and hit them hard on their head knocking them out. They took those unconscious guards inside the room.

There was a locker that was password protected. Kanha opened a password hacking device but he said it would take a minimum 10-15 mins to decrypt the password and open the locker.

Till then Vivaant took his time to hack Tarak's personal computer and found files of research related to Mt Kailash. Vivaant found the files and he quickly downloaded them and transferred it to his pen drive.

He found some folder with files named Dr Vishwanath. There were some videos where he saw his dad being tortured to get information on the box and on how to open the box.

He saw Tarak hold his hand over his dad's head and his hand was glowing and it was making Dr Vishwanath say whatever Tarak asked. He asked him about how to open the box. Dr Vishwanath was able to resist it a lot for a few times and later one day he finally broke down. Vivaant was furious, his rage for Tarak was increasing.

Vivaant found another security cam setup application and opened it. He saw his dad being held in a room secured by many guards.

By the time the password was cracked, Kanha was wearing his IR glasses to take the box out. He saw the

IR radiations in front of the box. Kanha tried to get the reflectors installed and took them out from his bag.

Vivaant looked at the box and wanted to quickly go and save his dad. So, he took out the box. Vivaant's action triggered the alarm. Now everyone was in danger.

"All guards are mobilized and are moving towards a room at the dead-end of the basement." Sukheshni informed over the earphones.

"That is where dad is kept hidden, I saw on the CCTV. I am going there." Vivaant told Kanha and Sukheshni over the earphone.

The head of the guards had called and informed Tarak. Tarak instructed them to secure Dr Vishwanath. Tarak did not think that someone might have broken into his office as it was highly secured.

Kanha noticed Vivaant's adrenaline was rushing through his veins. He knew his blood was boiling after watching those videos. Kanha for the first time saw the fiery eyes of Vivaant. He was rushing towards the room, Kanha held him and told him to calm down, "this is not the right time." Sukheshni echoed the same, "around 50 soldiers are surrounding the room so it is not the time."

Vivaant was not ready to listen. At any cost, he wanted to save his dad. "Vivaant you have Narasimha's rage in your eyes, which will destroy everything we have achieved till now; like Narasimha started destroying everything after he killed Hiranyakashipu. We should know when to control our emotions and thoughts. If we do not go out with this box and those files, we may not get your father out of this place. Before Tarak arrives here we have to get out." Kanha tried to calm Vivaant down.

Vivaant calmed down and listened to Kanha and tried to get out quietly. Kanha told Sukheshni to get out and go towards the vehicle before someone arrived.

Sukheshni went out, Vivaant and Kanha took the lift and came to the ground floor. Nobody was there as most of the guards were guarding the captive's room, they went towards the gate.

"I see a car coming towards the gate; it might be Tarak's," Sukheshni informed. Vivaant and Kanha disguised themselves as gate guards. They opened the gate as Tarak's car came in and they closed the gate and ran towards their Jeep and drove towards their secret camp.

Tretayuga

Prahalada became the king of Danavas and ruled judiciously for many years, He was a king who was honoured in all the lokas.

He maintained peace in all the three lokas. He was an ardent devotee of Vishnu and spent most of his life praying and teaching the world about the greatness of Vishnu.

Ikshvaku, the son of Manu was the King of Manavas who ruled at the time of Satyayuga. Ikshvaku and Prahalada were both peace lovers. They wanted their civilizations to grow beyond what they had achieved till now.

They wanted to facilitate people to travel beyond their planets and star system. So, they asked Vishwakarma to create portals to other stars, constellations and planets.

Vishwakarma sent his finest disciple, Maya to architect the stargates and portals on Bhuloka and Bhuvarloka. Maya was one of the greatest architects in the whole universe.

Maya discussed with Vishwakarma, Ikshvaku and Prahalada his plans of building stargates in the shape of pyramids.

Maya explained that to create stargates it has to hold lots of energy inside it and needs to be projected with that concentrated energy towards the Ionosphere to create a wormhole which in turn will open a tunnel between one stargate to another.

He had studied a lot of structures such as a sphere, cube, cuboid, spheroid and pyramid. When the energy was tried to be confined in these structures, there was a huge loss of energy in all the other structures except the pyramid where the energy loss was minimal.

Pyramids can hold 85% of energy. He wanted to build pyramids which could provide unlimited energy that could benefit the whole world.

Once these pyramids were built, people could travel to higher planets such as Mahar Loka in Lyra constellation and Janaloka, a planet of the great sages in Pleiades constellation.

To travel through the stargates, one must know that his body is made up of the panchabhutas. People should be aware of panchabhutas and activate all the Chakras which will help them to lead a healthy life.

Maya explained the design of the pyramids is such that they will enhance and emit radiations which correspond to the element of the panchabhutas such as Pruthvi, Varuna, Agni, Vayu and Vyoma.

For a Pyramid, to concentrate its energy it needs a lens to focus. An oval-shaped orb needs to be placed at the eye of the pyramid at the top portion and the oval-shaped orb can absorb all the energy and focus it and emit radiation.

The orb will decide which elements of panchabhutas it can focus and distribute to everyone seeking it on the whole planet.

For example, if a fire orb is placed at the eye of a pyramid, it would propel radiations with the frequency of Agni which will activate the Manipura chakra which will help people radiate prana throughout the body.

There are other two orbs which are special that correspond to soul and consciousness.

There are seven stones corresponding to seven chakras of the human body. When the pyramids emit these radiations massively, all humans will be benefitted from it as activating chakras will energize them and heal them from any ailments.

He showed his plans to build many pyramids all over the world which would activate all the seven chakras of the body on both Bhuloka and Bhuvarloka.

A Mahayogi who has activated all his chakras should be able to open the portal to travel through other planes.

The human body is made up of all the elements such as Pruthvi, Varuna, Agni, Vayu and Vyoma. Soul and consciousness make him a complete human being.

Once the portal is open, every cell in the human body vibrates at the natural frequency of all the elements and the body becomes one with the elements. The human body becomes the radiations and passes through the portal through the other side of the pyramid which will be another planet.

Vishwakarma felt proud of his disciple being able to plan and design all this. Prahalada and Ikshvaku extended their full support and said they would give any number of men that Maya needed to build those pyramids.

Tarak's office

Tarak entered his warehouse and was relieved to see that Dr Vishwanath was safe. He wondered who would have dared to break-in.

A thought crossed his mind; did somebody know about the secret box. He then assured himself that no one knew about it.

He then asked to see the CCTV footage. While watching the footage he saw three people coming in and two of them entering the lift. What he saw thereafter shocked him.

He saw two people were pulled off from the lift and those two guys went to the basement and then the alarm went off and after a few minutes, two people came out of the lift with the box being carried out.

He sensed something unthinkable had happened. He wondered how they knew about the box and who would have told them. He then realized that Dorjee was in Kanha's custody and this could have been his doing.

He suddenly stormed off to his room and opened the locker and saw that the box was missing. Coming out he shouted and asked who the guards at the gate were and how did they go out.

The guy who was monitoring the CCTV footage with Tarak came forward and said, "Sir, they were unconscious, the guards who opened the gates for you were the thieves. We saw that in the footage."

Tarak's frustration had crossed its limits. He called Devaant and took him to his office and closed the door.

Devaant watched the footage while Tarak said it could have been that Indian officer, Kanha who had held Dorjee captive. Devaant saw the Lapiz lazuli pendant on Vivaant and confirmed he was the son of Dr Vishwanath and might have been accompanied by Kanha and they had not left the country as they had guessed and the girl might be Sukheshni.

Army secret camp

Kanha was happy that he got the box. But Vivaant wasn't as he was not able to rescue his father.

Kanha reassured him that they would rescue Dr Vishwanath. But first, they had to finish his work, they had to know what Dr Vishwanath was trying to safeguard. They didn't know how to open the box.

Vivaant took the box. The box started emitting a blue light in the centre as his pendant was near the box. He took the pendant and inserted it at that place where it was shining and turned it like a key. It clicked, nothing worked. He tried many times turning the pendant from left to right, but the box didn't open.

He asked Sukheshni to bring her bracelet and when the bracelet came in the vicinity of the box, seven small holes started shining below the place where the pendant was inserted.

The holes started shining in the colours of the Rainbow. Sukheshni's bracelet had stones in the colours of VIBGYOR. Vivaant cut the bracelet and removed the stones, one by one and inserted them into the holes of their respective colours.

Once he inserted all the stones, he heard a hard clicking sound. Then he turned and inserted the pendant.

The box opened up with a few complex locks. Inside there were some old palm leaf manuscripts with something written in Sanskrit.

There was a diagram of a pyramid ejecting a beam of light from the top with an oval shaped orb at the eye of the pyramid and a lot of palm leaves were inscribed in Sanskrit.

Tarak's Office

Tarak was not looking unhappy, he was smiling at the happenings.

"Dad, why are you smiling?" Devaant who was shocked asked Tarak.

"The box has reached the right place. The box hasn't been opened for millenniums; it will now be opened. The secrets are easily accessible now. It's about time we get our hands over it." Tarak happily told Devaant.

Tretayuga

Succeeding Prahalada, his son Virochana ruled peacefully and after him, his son, Bali. He was an ambitious king, he was trained by Shukracharya himself to become the greatest warrior, his ambition should be to conquer all worlds.

Bali was always true to his word and an ardent devotee of Vishnu like his father and grandfather.

Once Bali was enthroned as king after Virochana, he took the whole army to Bhuloka through the pyramid's space portals and conquered Bhuloka without much bloodshed. He ensured that everyone lived happily.

Indra was feared by the strength of Bali. Kailash Parvat was able to open a huge gateway in which a whole army could be taken to Swargaloka even before Bali could come and lay siege to Swarga Loka. Indra went to Maharloka to ask for help from the Narasimhas and other humanoids who were settled there after Satyayuga.

Trivikrama Narasimha, the king of all humanoids said, "We will only defend our planet, we won't interfere in the three lokas. We have left that and settled here in Maharloka.

Indra was left with the only choice of asking for help from Vishnu by going to Vaikuntha. Vishnu said that Bali hadn't harmed anyone and was doing justice to everyone. "If he walks in the path of adharma only then will I stop him."

Indra tried to make peace with Bali and tried to fill his ears and mislead him by saying that the Manavas were leading a luxurious life in this environment and to get whatever he wanted through Bhuloka.

The Danavas, on the other hand, were always working hard and struggling. Indra advised him to bring the Danavas to Bhuloka to let them enjoy the resources here.

Bali forgot that the Manavas and Danavas were different in nature and couldn't live together happily. As the Danavas were strong, after coming to Bhuloka, they started hurting and dominating the Manavas.

After a few days, they started attacking ashrams and hurting rishi munis and their families. They began praying Vishnu to come and save them from the Danavas.

Bali was trying to maintain peace and take the rishi munis into confidence and do yaga and gift lands, jewels, and precious items to the Rishis to set up their ashram once again. Vishnu came to Earth disguised as Vamana; a dwarf human Brahmin when the yaga was being performed.

Bali asked, "Vamana Brahmin, please let me know what you need," Vamana asked Bali to do his thulabhara and give him whatever he could.

Bali agreed to do the thulabhara of Vamana. One side of the balance sat the great Vamana and Bali filled the other side with all gold and jewels he had but it didn't even shake.

Bali said, "I the king of all the three worlds weigh the weight of the whole Bhuloka in my hands," and tried to pull down the balance. It didn't even shake.

Then he told him he would weigh the whole weight of Swarga Loka on his right leg and tried to press it down. It shook a bit.

Bali realized that he was no ordinary man. He told him he would place the weight of all the three worlds with himself and he sat on the balance and prayed to Vishnu to give him the strength to satisfy the Brahmin's needs.

Then the balance came to the centre. Bali was pleased and asked him to show his true identity. Vishnu revealed his true identity. Bali kneeled and touched his feet and asked for his blessings.

"The whole universe is in you my lord. I am a fool who thought I could rule the three worlds peacefully, but I know I have failed miserably for you to come." Bali surrendered himself to Mahavishnu.

"Bali, you are the greatest king who tried to rule all three worlds peacefully. But let the Manavas and Danavas live in their worlds separately and happily." Vishnu said and blessed Bali to be the Indra of the next Manvantara.

Bali accepted the verdict and Vishnu made him the King of Sutala Loka.

Chapter 8

THE SEVEN CHAKRAS

Ashram

A few hours after all the yoga sessions were over; Guruji was meditating at his Dhyana Mandira when Kanha greeted him.

"Where are those kids? I was waiting for you three. Bring them and meet me in the library section," Guruji ordered Kanha.

Kanha was shocked as to how Guruji knew about this. But he followed Guruji's instructions and took Vivaant and Sukheshni to the library.

"May I look at the box?" Guruji smiled and asked. Everyone was stunned as to how Guruji knew about this.

"How do you know about the box?" asked Sukheshni unable to tolerate her curiosity.

"Someone informed me about your arrival but let's discuss it later." Guruji told them.

Guruji was astonished to see the findings in the secret box. He said, "These palm-leaf inscriptions are thousands of years old."

These inscriptions talk about the Kailash Parvat as a pyramid built by an ancient architect, Maya. Kailash is the biggest pyramid on Bhuloka with a perfect disguise hidden in the Himalayas.

The architect mentions this place leads to the city of gods, Swargaloka and other planets and star systems.

Kailash is known as the staircase to heaven in many beliefs. Maya tells the gateway to heaven can be opened only by a Mahayogi who has activated all his chakras.

Who can wield the powers once wielded by the Adiyogi Shiva? Only he can produce a frequency to open the gateway to other lokas.

It is written that the four faces of the pyramid are built of crystal, ruby, gold and lapis lazuli. There is a door which can be opened on the side of lapis lazuli. A Mahayogi can open the door to get inside the pyramid.

The energy of the pyramid needs to be concentrated and directed by:

One who is born in Vyoma

One who came and touched Pruthvi

One who ignited Agni

One who is shaped by Jal

One who is immovable by Vayu

One whose soul is Shiva himself

"We need to know what it is and solve this puzzle," said Guruji.

Everyone wondered what the script was speaking about and were expecting answers from Guruji but even he needed some time to resolve it as he was clueless for now.

"Who is he, who can direct this energy, can it be opened only by Shiva, like how he controlled and directed the flow of Ganga on the Earth?" asked Sukheshni.

"Definitely it says that the soul is of Shiva, but there are lot of other things which needs to be true," said Guruji.

"Okay, let us see one by one. What is born in Vyoma?" asked Vivaant.

"Outer space is filled with stars, planets, asteroids, meteors and the only thing which can come and touch pruthvi is a meteor," said Guruji.

"That makes sense, a meteor fall can sometimes ignite a fire in the forest because of the heat, right?" asked Sukheshni.

"Yes, but what is shaped by Jal?" wondered Vivaant.

"Now I get it!" exclaimed Guruji.

"What is it Guruji?" asked Sukheshni.

"The meteors which fall on the Earth, over a period of several years are formed into the shape of lingas in the rivers of Saraswati. Even in the present age, lingas found in the Narmada river are formed similarly. The Shivalinga is not movable by air and has the soul of Shiva himself.

Maybe the Shivalinga needs to be installed at the eye of the pyramid to open the portal gateway successfully," explained Guruji.

On further examination of the palm leaf scripts, Guruji revealed, "It is mentioned that the one who can open the portal can emit frequencies of fire, earth, space, water and wind can also be used to emit any such frequency to radiate energy throughout the body.

These radiations can help activate the chakras of all the people. A Mahayogi can chant the mantras to produce frequencies to match the frequencies produced by the orb to open the stargate by using which people can travel to any of the lokas.

122

No wonder there were so many yogis in the ancient age who activated all their chakras."

Vivaant asked, "What are these chakras? Are there stones that can emit frequencies of all the five elements and activate these chakras?"

"My child, there are seven chakras and each person should try to activate them.

The five elements from which all creation has manifested and their power are accessible through 'Chakras' located in the spinal area.

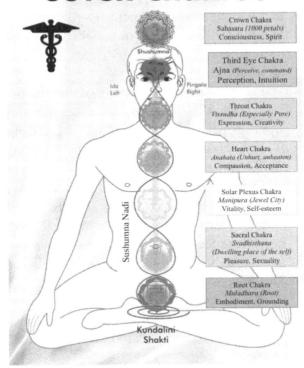

Seven Chakras

123

The chakras are energy centres in the astral body corresponding to the five locations in the spinal region and two in the area of the brain. Each chakra is endowed with the capacity to awaken certain powerful features.

The seven stones which are present on this pendant or the seven stones from the bracelet that you have inserted in this box to open represent the seven chakras.

- The Red stone represents Muladhara Chakra or Root Chakra. The positive attributes are good physical energy and vitality. It governs the functioning of the lower back, lower spine, kidneys and bladder. It indicates Pruthvi or Earth element.

- The Orange stone represents Swadishthana or Sacral Chakra and is characterized by flexibility and flow. It has connections with the pelvis and reproductive organs. It indicates Jala or Water element.

- The Yellow stone represents Manipura or Solar Plexus Chakra. It governs the digestive organs, stomach, pancreas, liver, middle back and muscles. It gives strength and energy. It indicates Agni or Fire element.

- The Green stone represents Anahata or Heart Chakra. It relates to the cardiac nerve, thymus gland, breasts, arms, shoulders, chest, lungs and heart. It represents love, empathy and compassion to all. It indicates Vayu or Air element.

- The Blue stone represents Vishuddha or Throat Chakra. It relates to palate, pharynx, tongue, jaws and mouth. It represents faith in ourselves, trust in others and creativity. It indicates Vyom or Space element.

- The Indigo stone represents Ajna or Third Eye Chakra. It has a strong relationship with the pineal gland. It relates to feeling, hearing and seeing. It will work on building your inner knowledge, inspiration and your true purpose. It indicates a light element or the soul.
- The Violet stone represents Sahasrara or Crown Chakra. It connects you to the universe. It relates to the cerebral cortex and the brain.

The energy of Crown Chakra allows you to experience mystical oneness with everything. There is peace, joy and happiness. It gives you a glimpse of other realities which are beyond your physical and material reality. It indicates the Thought element or Consciousness.

This is a brief introduction on Chakras. These can be activated in many ways like Yoga and Meditation. You can read more about them in the library".

Vivaant asked Guruji, "But which are the oval-shaped stones that can activate this and the space portal gateway to other planets."

Guruji said, "I need some time to search for it in the library."

Sukheshni said, "I can also help but I need a laptop so that I can search on the internet about them."

"Let us have breakfast and do this research. We will try to search for it in the library and the internet for answers," said Guruji.

After a while, everyone started doing their research to know more about the orbs. A little later, Sukheshni said that she had found something and had studied on it. She called everyone and spoke about a theory that she had arrived at.

"I feel these were the Shivalingas which were brought to life by the Tapas Shakti of Adiyogi Shiva that can emit the frequencies of Panchabhutas.

These five Shivalingas which were first put to life are placed in the same longitude i.e., 79° east.

Pruthvilinga which can activate Muladhara Chakra is at Kanchipuram and the linga is Ekambareshwara.

Jalalinga which can activate Swadishthana Chakra is at Thiruvanaikkaval and the linga is Jambukeshwara.

Agnilinga which can activate Manipura Chakra is at Thiruvannamalai and the linga is Arunachaleshwara.

Vayulinga which can activate Anahata Chakra is at Kalahasti and the linga is Srikalahastheshwara.

Akashalinga which can activate Muladhara Chakra is at Chidambaram and the linga is Nataraja.

But I am not sure about the other two lingas which can stimulate the Ajna Chakra which in turn can activate and heal our Atma and the Sahasra Chakra which activates and heals our consciousness."

Guruji explained further, "The linga which can energize our consciousness can let our Panchabhutas, soul and consciousness to travel throughout the other planes and space to other planets and star systems."

"I have heard a story where Shiva gave his Atma linga to Ravana and it was installed at Gokarna by Ganesha," said Vivaant.

"Yes, that might be the Shivalinga which can activate the Ajna Chakra. But only Shiva knows where the last Shivalinga is hidden. There are thousands of Shivalingas. Where will we find it?"

"Only a Mahayogi who has activated all the chakras by Tapas or Yoga can activate the Kailash portal and Tarak is one such person," Guruji revealed.

"How do you know that?" asked Vivaant with surprise.

"Twenty years ago, we were all students of a Mahayogi where we activated our chakras at the Saptharishi cave near Kailash Parvat. At that time, we were three - myself, Tarak and my dear friend, Dr Vishwanath," said Guruji.

Vivaant exclaimed, "Dad!!! You know my dad?"

Guruji was surprised, "You know Dr Vishwanath?"

"Yes, he is my father. We were in search of him and now found out that Tarak has held him captive. You said that you all know each other but he held him for this box," Vivaant was looking for answers from Guruji.

Guruji sighed! "Tarak is a person who can do anything to achieve what he wants. Now I will tell you how I knew that you guys would come with the box. Tarak had come here early this morning and said that you guys stole the box from him and if you don't return it to him, he will destroy this ashram and let the Chinese Government know that Kanha is still working undercover. He has CCTV footage on how Kanha entered his building and took this secret box. If he discloses it. It will lead to tension at the the border."

Vivaant hit his fist to his hand, "How can we give this information to Tarak? If this goes into the wrong hands, the Earth might be under threat. If somehow Tarak opens the portal to other planets and star systems, aliens can come and attack us. It is not safe but what will Tarak gain from this? What is his intention? What does he want to achieve?".

Guruji said retaining his calm, "I am afraid, I am also not aware of that my child. I know you guys have taken a lot of effort to get this box and don't want to hand it over to a dangerous person but in the interest of national security of India, we should do it. We should learn from the great King Maha Bali who gave up everything he had earned when the situation demanded it,".

"He has waited for twenty years for this box and is ready to do anything to lay his hands on it. So, we can bargain for the release of Dr Vishwanath while we handover this." Kanha asked Guruji if they could do this deal, they could take care of the box later.

"Sounds like a good idea, I'll try and speak to Tarak over this and get my dear old friend back." Guruji assured Kanha and Vivaant.

"By that time, I'll try and make arrangements to safely handover this to Tarak. Guruji by then please let us know the place," said Kanha.

Guruji spoke on the telephone in his room and returned.

"Tarak has agreed to our demands and said that you guys should go to the place where his helipad is located. He will come there with Dr Vishwanath. He has asked me to tell that you guys will have to come at midnight when clock strikes 12," Guruji informed Kanha.

"My child, You can stay here and continue your research to find the last linga, I will be there if you need any help" Guruji assured Sukheshni.

Kanha asked Sukheshni to stay with Guruji. Kanha and Vivaant left with the box to the rendezvous suggested by Tarak.

Tarak's office

"They are coming with the box near the helipad, take your team. They are swapping the box for Dr Vishwanath. Fetch the box and tell your boys to finish them all." Tarak instructed Devaant over the call.

"Once we get hold of the box there is no reason to simply kill them and make big news about it," Devaant opined.

"Do you think Kanha is a fool that he will allow you to take the box easily with you?" Tarak said.

Devaant tried interrupting, "But Dad!" Tarak shut him up and curtly said, "Just do as I say."

Devaant went to the place where Dr Vishwanath had been kept. He had never gone to that place to see him.

Whenever Devaant saw from the cameras, Dr Vishwanath was not opening his mouth and never gave any expressions how much ever they tortured him. He always kept his calm.

Devaant went inside the room and asked the guards to untie him from the chair. Devaant went near Dr Vishwanath. He did not understand those expressions.

Dr Vishwanath did not look worried. He was making sounds as if he wanted to speak to him but his mouth was plastered and hands were tied behind him.

As he went nearer, tears rolled down the eyes of Dr Vishwanath. Devaant didn't care. He said, "Be happy you are going to get liberated from here today." Devaant felt sorry for him being in prison for two decades as it was not an easy thing.

Devaant pushed him towards the security guards and directed them to take him to the Jeep. Dr Vishwanath turned back with teary eyes and looked towards Devaant. The guards took him to the Jeep, Devaant went and sat in the Jeep and left for the helipad.

Near Helipad

Kanha and Vivaant were standing there waiting for Tarak. But Devaant showed up with Dr Vishwanath.

Kanha came forward with the box and told Devaant to release Dr Vishwanath who was still in tears but was in shock to see the box was with a man and it was open.

Dr Vishwanath was worried; he knew the intention of Tarak. Vishwanath was trying to tell Kanha not to hand it over. Kanha understood his concern but ignored him.

Devaant asked the guards to release Dr Vishwanath and moved towards Kanha to get the box. Dr Vishwanath moved forward and Vivaant came towards his father.

As Devaant collected the box he signalled his team to start firing as soon as he finishes verification of the box. Vivaant went and hugged his father in excitement and told him, "Dad! It's me Vivaant your younger son."

Dr Vishwanath was happy that at least he was in the arms of one of his sons.

Vivaant started untying him and removed the plaster from his mouth. Lhawang and the team who had hovered around the place started moving in from their hiding places while everyone was busy.

Dr Vishwanath told Vivaant that the box was important and not to let it fall into Tarak's hands or else he would bring hell down on Earth. Vivaant didn't understand anything. Vishwanath said one more thing which shook Vivaant. "Go stop your brother!" Vivaant exclaimed "Brother?" "Yes, he is your elder brother, Vedaant, he doesn't know that," said Dr Vishwanath.

Kanha came back and was trying to get them to safety. Devaant sat in the Jeep and instructed his team to finish them off.

Lhawang and his team of officers started firing towards Devaant's team. They got scrambled by the unexpected shooting by Lhawang and his team. Devaant quickly asked his driver to move the Jeep and escaped while his guards gave him cover.

As one of the guards from Devaant's team was firing at them, Vishwanath saw someone from Vivaant's side was firing at Vivaant.

Vishwanath sidelined him and took the bullets meant for Vivaant. Lhawang shot that person instantly. Vivaant's world stopped for a second. He shouted "Dad! Dad! Why did you do this?" he started crying.

Dr Vishwanath smiled and said, "Looks like I have already lost one son, didn't want to lose another."

Vivaant said, "Nothing will happen to you, we will take you to a hospital."

Kanha, Vivaant and Lhawang took Vishwanath to the Jeep and drove away quickly to get medical attention.

Tears rolled down Vivaant's cheeks. Holding his father's hand, he pleaded, "Please don't leave me again.".

"My time has come my child, please take care of your mother and apologize to her on my behalf." Vishwanath tried hard to look at Vivaant with his blurry eyes.

Lhawang cursed himself for not getting enough security. "I apologize Kanha, bringing any help from air was too risky. This was all I could arrange even after you had tipped me off."

"Don't blame yourselves officers, you guys don't know whom you are stacked against. For Tarak, getting that secret is everything that he has ever aimed for. He has trained my own son against me," Vishwanath spoke not withstanding his throbbing pain as blood started oozing out of his bullet injuries.

Kanha didn't want to but asked, "Sir, I am sorry to ask this question now, but did you decode the inscriptions on the palm leaves? Which is the Shivalinga and where is it located?"

Vishwanath said that the last time somebody knew about it was Sri Krishna when he hid it to save Earth from the Danavas. Vishwanath turned towards Vivaant and said, "It looks like you guys have already figured out most of it."

Vivaant said, "Your friend Lieutenant Ponnappa's daughter Sukheshni helped us to decode it."

132

It was hard to stop the bleeding even with the tight cloth tied around. Vishwanath was a yogi, he held on for a bit longer.

"Son, it looks like my time has come. Don't tell all this to your mom. She will again feel the loss of her husband. We should not dig up her buried pain. You take good care of her. Promise me that you will save your brother from the evil clutches of Tarak. Give your mother her elder son back whom I had taken from her. Please fulfil my last wish," Dr Vishwanath took a pledge from his son.

Vivaant was crying and assured, "No dad, nothing will happen to you. I will save you."

Vishwanath said, "I am sorry son; I could not be with you while you were growing up but I am lucky to have you beside me when I am dying." He closed his eyes and his soul left for the higher worlds in peace.

There was no stop to Vivaant's cries. He didn't know whether he should be angry at his own brother that he had ordered the killing of his father or feel pity for him as he didn't know who he was.

Kanha tried to console him and said, "Vivaant, control yourself. Your dad needs to be given proper death rites, he has martyred for the nation.

We will make a case to the Indian Government that you were kidnapped from the trip and we found Dr Vishwanath dead and ask that you guys be sent back to India.

I think officer Lhawang can help us in putting a word to the Tibetan Government."

Kanha called and informed Guruji what had happened and requested to send Sukheshni to Lhawang's office.

"It's disheartening to hear what happened to my friend Vishwanath. But its the way of life. Did Vishwanath knew about the linga?" enquired guruji after expressing his grief.

"Not exactly, But he pointed towards Shri Krishna hiding it somewhere to save Earth from the Danavas." answering guruji's question Kanha disconnected the call.

Lhawang made the necessary arrangements to send Vivaant, Sukheshni and Dr Vishwanath's body.

Sirkha

Colonel Veerprathap welcomed them on the other side of the border with teary eyes and hugged Vivaant and took them to the Army base camp. The Colonel asked Vivaant, "Do you want to call your mom for the final rites of your father?"

"No, it was my dad's last wish not to tell anything to mom about this. He didn't want to dig up her 20-year-old pain. Let's carry out my father's final rites today," said Vivaant.

"Kanha will be here soon. He has aborted the mission and returned which he should have done earlier but stayed because of you guys," the Colonel told Vivaant.

Kanha came back and as planned everyone went and buried Dr Vishwanath according to his family custom. Kanha knew Vivaant was in a lot of grief. So, he took him to a room at the army camp.

Vivaant began sobbing again, "Everything is over, my dad died in my arms and I could not do anything."

Kanha said, "I will tell you a story of Sri Ramachandra and Hanuman. Hanuman was so protective of Sri Rama that even the God of Death, Yama never dared take Rama when his time on Earth was over.

One day Rama's ring fell into a hole inside the palace. Rama asked Hanuman to fetch the ring for him. Hanuman went in search of the ring and saw a hole.

He became small as a bee and entered the hole and ended up in Patala Loka, the underground city which was ruled by Ahiravana and guarded by Makharadwaja.

As Hanuman went to the underground city, a reptilian, Makharadwaja stopped him. Hanuman asked, "Who are you?" The reptilian said, "I am the son of Hanuman." Hanuman replied, "I am Hanuman and I am a Brahmachari and I take no wife and I have no children."

Makharadwaja said, "I am born to a Makara. When you burned the whole of Lanka, out of the heat and your energy, your sweat dropped into the ocean. That initiated the release of an egg from a makara, my mother. Thus, I am born with your strength. Forgive me for stopping you. May I ask what have you come for?"

Hanuman asked, "Who is the ruler of this underground city and how did you come here?"

Makharadwaja said, "This is ruled by Ahiravana, the brother of Maha Ravana who was killed by Sri Rama who found me on the shores of Lanka while he was returning. He trained me and made me the guardian of this place."

Hanuman said, "Okay, I intend to meet him. Prabhu Sri Ram's ring fell to the Patala and I came in search of it."

Hanuman met Ahiravana and explained why he had come. Ahiravana smiled and said, "So, It is true?" Hanuman asked, "What is true?"

Ahiravana asked, "Okay, before I show you the ring I want to know about Sri Ram and his greatness, he was the one who defeated my brother, the great Ravana." Hanuman explained about the greatness of Sri Ram.

Ahiravana showed Hanuman the room where the ring had fallen. Hanuman saw a huge pile of rings and asked, "All rings are the same, which one is Sri Ram's?"

Ahiravana said, "Every one of them is Sri Ram's. There is a story about this place and I came to know it is true today."

Hanuman asked, "What is the story?"

Ahiravana said, "At the end of every descending Tretayuga, a Vanara comes in search of the ring and his master departs from the Bhuloka."

Hanuman was shocked and went towards Sri Ram's palace and while he was travelling, he knew that this cycle of life goes on in every Mahayuga and Sri Ram would come again and he couldn't stop it from happening.

Kanha told Vivaant, "Even our God Hanuman could not stop death, who are we? This cycle of life should go on and we should move forward, we can't control life and death."

Vivaant finally fell silent and said, "I get that Kanha, but I need time to get over it."

"I know it's been hard for you. Go home to your mother and be with her. It's all over now. We don't know what is Tarak's plan; we shall try to find out and try to stop him. I will try to save your brother." Kanha advised Vivaant.

"It's my father's last wish. I have to fulfill it to give peace to my father's soul. I have to fulfill my responsibilities as a son and as a brother too. I have to take my brother to my mom and show him that he has a family." Vivaant stood firm in his decisions.

"I understand Vivaant, I respect your decisions let's talk about it later, now take some rest." Kanha closed the door.

Chapter 9

DWAPARAYUGA

In Tretayuga, Rama punished most of the Danavas who tried to hurt the Manavas or Rishi munis who were performing havans which made the Devas stronger who in turn, gave prosperity to Earth. During Rama's reign, the Danavas did not harm the Rishis and Manavas.

Once Rama left the Earth, Banasura, the son of Bali who was the king of Danavas thought that before trying to conquer Bhuloka he had to have allies on Bhuloka.

Banasura was able to travel to Bhuloka from Rasalinga provided by Vishwakarma which was made of solidified mercury which was placed in a pyramid on Mars. It would open a tunnel to a wormhole the other end of which would open at Kailash Parvat.

King Ugrasena and Padmavati of Vrishni Kingdom had a male child. But Banasura killed the child and replaced it with a small child of the Danava clan - the son of Kalanemi and the grandson of Hiranyaksha. Ugrasena and Padmavati named him Kamsa, the prince of Mathura.

Banasura tried to find allies on Bhuloka. He knew someone he could trust as he was reborn by the power of the Danava woman, Jara. Banasura met Jarasandha and outlined his plan to rule the whole of Bhuloka.

As Kamsa grew old, Jarasandha of Magadha married his daughter on the instructions of Banasura.

Kamsa, Jarasandha and Banasura had become allies and they had conquered most parts of Bharath. Banasura slowly started bringing the Danavas to Bhuloka.

It was time for Vishnu to stop this chaos caused by the Danavas on Bhuloka. He took birth as the son of Vasudeva and Devaki, the sister of Kamsa and the daughter of Ugrasena.

Kamsa was killing all the sons of Devaki. He did not want any contenders for the throne. He knew Ugrasena did not like him and still had every chance of handing over the throne to any male born of his blood.

When his eighth child was born, Vasudeva left him with his friends Nanda and Yashoda without the knowledge of Kamsa.

When the eighth child, Krishna grew up, the trio of Kamsa, Jarasandha and Banasura were busy conquering kingdoms. Kamsa somehow found out that the eighth son of Vasudeva and Devaki was still alive and asked the help of Banasura to bring the Danavas to Bhuloka through Kailasa to kill Krishna.

Kamsa sent Putana to kill Krishna when he was still a baby. She disguised herself as a beautiful lady and tried to kill him by breastfeeding him poison. But Krishna sucked the life out of her.

When Krishna was one-year old, Trinavarta, a Danava tried to kill him by bringing a great cyclone on Vrindavan but Krishna killed him. During his childhood, Krishna killed many Danavas like Aghasura, Bakasura, Vritrasura, Aristasura, Keshi, Vyomasura and many more.

Kamsa became frustrated with Krishna. To punish him he tortured Vasudeva and Devaki.

Krishna came to Mathura with his brother, Balarama where Kamsa was king on the invitation of Akrura for a yaga being carried out by him.

Kamsa sent his close aide, Chanura to kill them at Akrura's place. However, Krishna killed Chanura and went to the palace and took a head-on duel with Kamsa while Balarama fought a duel with Kamsa's brother Sunama.

Both Kamsa and Sunama were killed in the duel. After that, Krishna and Balarama freed Vasudeva, Devaki and Ugrasena who were jailed by Kamsa after he had overthrown him with the help of Banasura. Ugrasena declared that the kingdom belonged to Krishna from then on. Thus Krishna became the ruler of Mathura.

Army Camp

Kanha called for a meeting with the Colonel, Vivaant and Sukheshni and advised Vivaant and Sukheshni, "Tell your mothers that you will come in a few days as you are extending your trip. We have to first stop Tarak from reactivating the stargate at Kailash Parvat."

Vivaant said, "Dad mentioned that Tarak would bring 'hell on earth' what does that mean?"

Kanha said, "I don't know what that means. It might mean to open the gateway to hell or bring death to the people on Earth. By opening the gateway, he might expose the Earth to many dangers."

The Colonel remarked saying, "We do not know what to expect from extraterrestrials, we might not be able to tackle them. But to open the gateway as it was written on palm scripts, it should be open from both sides even if Tarak opens from here on Earth, who will open it from the other side? Tarak might be in contact with extraterrestrials on another planet."

Kanha asked, "But for that Tarak needs the Shivalinga, which no one knows where it is or does he know it already?"

"But uncle told us that only Krishna knew where he placed it. It means Krishna closed it for some reason. We have to find the reason, we should be able to decode Tarak's intention," opined Sukheshni.

"For that, we need to do some research and find some ancient scriptures," said Kanha.

The Colonel said, "When Dr Vishwanath was here, he had some books which I have packed and kept it in his trunk, you guys can search in them."

"Yes uncle, that will certainly be helpful. I will study them and try to find some answers." Sukheshni was ready to read them and find the missing pieces.

Vivaant and Sukheshni called their mothers and said they had finished their Kailash trip and were staying at a friend's place in Delhi.

They would finish sightseeing and return to Bangalore and they were together and assured them of their safety.

After Sukheshni started reading the books, Vivaant accompanied Kanha for physical training. Kanha trained him in shooting and to use all his gadgets and cautioned him to be always aware of what's happening around.

"Concentrate on your aim and you will achieve it," Kanha instructed Vivaant.

Vivaant clarified his view, "My main aim is to take my brother back to my mother to fulfil my father's last wish. I don't want his soul to have any unfulfilled wishes or any pain that he had separated a son from his mother. My mother has hated him forever for that."

Tarak's Office

Tarak appreciated Devaant who had finally got him what he needed; he had found the box. Devaant too was happy.

Tarak got the palm leaf scriptures. He asked Devaant to go and take rest.

Devaant said, "No, I want to see and know about this secret. We had to put in tons of effort to know what secret it holds about Mt Kailash."

Tarak strictly said, "It's none of your business, just follow what I said. Now leave me alone. I have to speak to our boss alone."

Devaant was also angry and asked, "I have taken so much risk to get this box, why don't you introduce me to your boss? I am your only son who manages this whole empire of Dhithi group of companies."

Tarak calmly replied, "Time will come for everything, now it is not the time. Please leave now." Devaant was disappointed and simply left to take care of other things."

Tarak again went to his secret room in the office and called requesting to meet his king, The King of Danavas, Simhanada.

King Simhanada's 3D hologram appeared and Tarak happily exclaimed, "Your Highness we have finally opened the box and the secrets have been revealed!"

But Simhanada didn't seem to be happy. Tarak was surprised. He asked Tarak, "Who are all aware about this box?"

Though he was scared, Tarak confidently said, "No one, Your Highness."

Simhanada thundered, "Don't lie to me, Tarakasura. I know from sources that officials of the Indian Government and another son of Dr Vishwanath opened it and they know the secrets too.

We should open the gateway before they know how to close it. But I am pleased that at least we possess the box now. Will you be able to open the gates? I'll get my armies prepared."

"Worry not my Lord, Everything will be executed as per my plan. One last piece of the puzzle is missing, I have assigned the task to the right person and will get the results soon." replied Tarak.

Simhanada said, "All the Best, Do it as soon as possible" After saying these words Simhanada's 3D hologram disappeared.

Chapter 10

KEY TO KAILASH

Mathura

Krishna ruled Mathura and relieved all of its citizens from the torture of Kamsa. Banasura on the other hand was losing all his allies and had a reason to be frustrated at Krishna.

Banasura planned to kill Krishna who was becoming a big headache. He called his close aide Dantavakra from Bhuvarloka.

Dantavakra went to the Chedi Kingdom disguised as a Maharshi. The Chedi King, Damaghosha and Queen Shrutashrava, sister of Vasudeva did not have a child. Dantavakra gave her a potion and asked her to take it saying that she would beget a strong son.

As the queen took that potion after a few months, a son was born who had an extra growth near the hands and eyes. He was named Shishupala. Shrutashrava was very sad.

When Vasudeva and Krishna came to see Shrutashrava, Krishna knew that he was a Danava but by seeing his aunt unhappy he made Shishupala normal and treated him.

While Shishupala was growing up, he was jealous of Krishna, as everyone was always praising him. Dantavakra became his guru who trained him and always taught him to become strong like Krishna so that he could defeat him one day. He told Banasura and Jarasandha that he would help in killing Krishna.

Krishna knew what was happening. He wanted to curb the Danavas on Bhuloka but he knew he had to first close the entrance to Bhuloka from other lokas which was Kailash Parvat. But first, he had to stop Banasura, Jarasandha, Dantavakra and Shishupala. It was important to stop Jarasandha first as he had conquered all the kings and had attacked Mathura after Kamsa was killed by Krishna.

Krishna and Balarama shifted their kingdom to Dwarka as they didn't want any harm to befall their subjects.

After Krishna helped the Pandavas to win the Kurukshetra battle, Yudhishthira started the Rajasuya yagna. Jarasandha didn't agree to Yudhishthira being king.

So, Bhima went with an army to Magadha. He challenged Jarasandha to a duel. Jarasandha swore he would kill Bhima and Krishna later.

Jarasandha was too strong to be defeated in a wrestling duel. Krishna knew Jarasandha was reborn by a Danava woman named Jara who had joined him from two splits of his body.

So, he instructed Bhima to split him apart. Bhima did so and killed Jarasandha and freed ninety-five kings who were captured by him.

Banasura was crestfallen. Krishna was killing all of his allies one by one. After Yudhishthira's yaga concluded, all the kings came to him.

Banasura provoked Shishupala that Krishna had killed their great ally Jarasandha with the help of Bhima. Now the world was praising him.

Shishupala came to the yaga and started insulting Krishna saying that he cheated Jarasandha by helping

Bhima and it wasn't a fair duel. Shishupala invited Krishna for a duel. He had got a lot of weapons from Banasura. There was a big battle where Shishupala used weapons which were used by the Danavas that stunned many kings. Krishna took his Sudarshana Chakra and killed Shishupala.

Dantavakra had brought up Shishupala like his own son. So, he went and attacked Krishna on his way back to Dwarka. Krishna killed him with his Sudarshana Chakra.

This relieved Jaya Vijaya of their three births as Vishnu's enemies who were cursed by the four Kumaras, the manasaputras of Brahma to have three births as Vishnu's enemies or hundred births as his devotees as normal beings.

Jaya Vijaya had chosen for three rebirths to come and join Vishnu faster. The first birth was being born as Hiranyaksha and Hiranyakashipu and the second birth was of Ravana and Kumbhakarna, the third and final was of Shishupala and Dantavakra.

Banasura was alone here on Bhuloka. He decided once and for all that he would battle with Krishna with all his might. Banasura was a capable and great warrior and a Mahayogi too.

He went to Kailash Parvat and activated the stargate and invited his greatest Danava warrior king and his closest ally, Shalva to come, attack and conquer Bhuloka.

The Danavas had a specialized war vimana called Saubha, which was built by Maya.

Shalva brought the whole Danava army with all weaponized space crafts from Bhuvarloka. Banasura and

Shalva attacked Dwarka. There was a great battle with Vrishnis and the warriors of Dwarka.

Note: The Srimad Bhagavatam mentions about the aircraft which Shalva used.

sa labdhva kama-gam yanam
tamo-dhama durasadam
yayas dvaravatim salvo
vairam vrsni-krtam smaran

– Srimad Bhagavatam 10.76.8

Translation: This unassailable vehicle was filled with darkness and could go anywhere. Upon obtaining it, Shalva, remembering the Vrishnis' enmity toward him, proceeded to the city of Dwarka.

Shalva fired thunderbolts from the Saubha Vimana on Dwarka thereby decimating all the buildings, palaces and the walls which surrounded the city and its gardens. Krishna could not intercept it, as the spacecraft was moving so fast that it was appearing and disappearing at a fast pace.

Note: The Srimad Bhagavatam mentions how Earth was tormented by Saubha.

ity ardyamana saubhena
krsnasya nagari bhrsam
nabhyapadyata sam rajams
tri-purena yatha mahi

– Srimad Bhagavatam 10.76.12

Translation: The city of Krishna thus terribly tormented by Saubha could, just as the Earth with Tripura, find no peace.

From Saubha, Shalva fired a bevy of missiles towards Krishna' chariot. Krishna avoided all the missiles. Then

Shalva fired a missile as big as a meteor, Krishna counter fired his nuclear weapon. The clash of the weapons in the space lit up the whole sky, the sound thundered in the ears of everyone. All went blind for a few minutes.

Pradyumna, son of Krishna and Rukmini accompanied by his brothers wearing the armor, mounted the chariots and went to fight against Shalva's army.

Pradyumna took on a head-to-head battle with Dyuman, Commander-in-chief of Shalva's army. Pradyumna was a master archer and he aimed at the rotary wings of Dyuman's aircraft and shattered them. Dyuman came down and mounted a chariot and attacked Pradyumna. Pradyumna's arrows destroyed the wheels of Dyuman's chariot. Pradyumna's arrows fortified with mantras decimated the weapons fired by Dyuman.

Pradyumna's arrow took Dyuman's crown and brought it to his feet. Pradyumna asked him to surrender. Dyuman jumped out of his broken chariot and rushed towards Pradyumna to attack with his mace. Pradyumna shot an arrow to his chest, Dyuman was thrown back a few yards by the impact and died.

The illusion created by Saubha made it very difficult for Krishna to hit. Saubha moved so fast that it created an illusory effect that Saubha appeared in hundreds of places in the sky.

Krishna took his bow and chanted a mantra and fixed an arrow on to his bow and shot at Saubha. The arrow multiplied itself into hundreds of arrows and hit each and every illusion created by Saubha and broke it. One of the arrows struck Saubha on his rotatory vimana engine and as it came down Krishna shattered Saubha with his club.

Note: The Srimad Bhagavatam mentions the battle between Shalva and Krishna.

> *tam sastra-pugaih praharantam ojasa*
> *salvam saraih saurir amogha-vikramah*
> *viddhvacchinad varma dhanuh siro-manim*
> *saubham ca satror gadaya ruroja ha*

– Srimad Bhagavatam 10.77.33

Translation: While Shalva continued to hurl torrents of weapons at Him with great force, Lord Krishna, whose prowess never fails, shot His arrows at Shalva, wounding him and shattering his armor, bow and crest jewel. Then with His club the Lord smashed His enemy's Saubha airship.

> *tat krsna-hasteritaya vicurnitam*
> *papata toye gadaya sahasradha*
> *visrjya tad bhu-talam asthito gadam*
> *udyamya salvo 'cyutam abhyagad drutam*

– Srimad Bhagavatam 10.77.34

Translation: Shattered into thousands of pieces by Lord Krishna's club, the Saubha vimana plummeted into the water. Shalva abandoned it, stationed himself on the ground, took up his club and rushed towards Lord Achyuta.

Shalva came down by parachute after Saubha was slaughtered and fell into the sea. Many of his warriors too came down. There was a battle on the ground. Shalva and his men came down and killed many of the Vrishnis.

Krishna came and hit Shalva with his mace. Shalva hit him back as hard as he could, Krishna tackled him. Krishna hit Shalva's chin from below with his mace. Shalva fell backwards on the stones at the beach and broke his head.

By the time Krishna could attack Banasura, he fled with his remaining army along with his spaceship to Bhuvarloka; the gateway was still open.

Krishna followed him to Kailasha but by that time Banasura and his army had fled. While Banasura was closing the gate, Krishna sent a Brahmastra through the gateway which destroyed the atmosphere on Mars or Bhuvarloka. So, the Danavas went on to live in the underground cities of Bhuvarloka.

Krishna wanted to stop it once for all. He reached the eye of the pyramid and brought the Shivalinga which helped open the gateway to Dwarka.

Note: Evidence has been found on Mars of nuclear explosions. Xenon isotopes found in abundance on the surface of Mars provides proof that there were nuclear explosions on Mars in the past.

Army Camp

Sukheshni did her research and got a breakthrough. She called Vivaant, Kanha and Colonel Veerprathap.

They all assembled in the Colonel's office where no one else was allowed.

Sukheshni began, "I have done the research and discussed it with guruji over the phone and guruji has validated my theory. We know that Krishna took the linga and hid it somewhere. I read a story which might be helpful. In Srimad Bhagavatam, Shalva and Krishna fought in Dwarka with deadly weapons and spacecrafts with the help of Danavas.

Shalva destroyed half of Dwarka and Krishna routed them back after killing Shalva from Kailash Parvat with the Brahmastra. He destroyed the Danava Loka and returned to Dwarka.

It means when the Danavas were routed back, Krishna closed the gateway of Mt. Kailash. Krishna might have taken the linga back to Dwarka."

The Colonel said, "There is a linga in Dwarka, i.e., Nageshwara Jyotirlinga in Dwarka, Gujarat. We might have to secure it."

"No uncle, a decade ago archaeologists found an ancient city submerged in the ocean in Gulf of Khambat that is referred to as the original Dwarka which is over 5000 years old. This was submerged when Krishna left the Earth in 3102 BC," Sukheshni interrupted him.

Vivaant said, "If the entire city is submerged then the Shivalinga might also be submerged and safe. I have heard legends saying Krishna asked the ocean to submerge Dwarka. He might have done it to save the Earth from these threats and submerge the secrets along with the city."

"You may be correct Vivaant, but there is an important story I found out about how Krishna and Balarama left this planet." After Krishna returned to Dwarka all the Vrishnis had died. The curse of Gandhari had come true; Krishna's lineage was finished like that of the Kaurava clan.

Krishna decided to leave this planet Earth. An arrow shot by a hunter named Jara struck his toe at the end of Dwaparayuga," Sukheshni continued.

Vivaant asked, "What does it signify?"

Sukheshni said, "It's not about how he died but where he died. It was near the Somnath temple. After he died, the land till Somnath temple is submerged but not Somnath.

Balarama left his body and became Adishesha and went near a cave close to Somnath temple to probably protect the linga. It is even said that Krishna built this temple with wood.

Later, the Chalukyan King, Mularaja renovated it before 997 AD. Ghazni attacked the temple so many times to loot and as we know he destroyed the Shivalinga. But there is a different story about Ghazni here in these files, we should all observe carefully.

When he tried to attack the Shivalinga and entered the garbhagudi all their weapons and armor wearing soldiers began to float and Ghazni was stunned by this.

One of his close aides said that there might be lodestones which act as a magnet in the upper gopura and below the floor which makes the Shivalinga and the iron levitate.

Ghazni first ordered demolition of the gopura and then the linga fell to the ground and then a soldier tried to destroy the linga but couldn't, due to being in such a strong magnetic field it had begun to act like a magnet.

All weapons made of iron were of no use. So Ghazni told them to bury it there and later to get fame, he broke some other linga and sent it to Mecca and Madina glorifying it.

When Sardar Vallabhai Patel ordered excavation, they found the original Shivalinga buried below the sanctum of the temple. He ordered that it not be disclosed to anyone and he installed the original Shivalinga again."

Sukheshni read from the files and said, "It is written in the secret files which Dr Vishwanath possessed."

"My gut feeling says this Shivalinga might be attacked again and we should not let history repeat itself." Sukheshni said.

Vivaant said, "If Krishna rerouted the army of Danavas and the gate was closed for them, then Tarak might be helping to open a gateway for the Danavas. They might be waiting to take revenge but why is Tarak helping them."

Kanha said, "Maybe he is one of them. Everyone fell silent and thought about it. I had researched a lot about Tarak. There is absolutely no record of him anywhere; he was what he was doing 20 years ago. No birth record, no education record. Locals mentioned they had UFO sightings twenty years ago. Maybe he is a Danava."

Sukheshni asked, "If they have UFOs, why do they need the gateway when they can travel in space?"

Kanha said, "Maybe to bring a whole army. It is not feasible in spacecrafts. Even in spacecrafts this is the shortest distance. They can bring thousands of Danavas in a short time."

Tarak's Office

Tarak called Devaant and told him that they must steal a Shivalinga from Dwarka. Devaant exclaimed, "Dwarka! Are you out of your mind? How to steal a whole Shivalinga and that too from Dwarka, are you crazy? Which temple do you want me to steal it from?"

Tarak replied saying, "I have done some research. It is from a temple which Krishna built, it is called Somnath temple."

"But why?" asked Devaant, "Is this related to Mt. Kailash? Now I need to know why we have to do this?"

Tarak said, "Don't question me, just do as I say. Don't mess up. Take a team and replace the Shivalinga with a stone replica and bring that Shivalinga to me."

"But it's a big temple and there will be a lot of security. If we disturb anything, the police force could come there," said Devaant.

Tarak retorted, "Don't give excuses. If you cannot do it, I will send someone else."

Devaant responded by saying, "No, it's okay I'll do it but promise me you will tell me the secrets and introduce me to the Boss."

"Yes, I will think about it and make arrangements but first finish this task." Devaant took his team of professionals and left for Lucknow.

Lhawang called Kanha and informed him that he had been tracking Devaant and Tarak. Devaant and a set of people were coming to India and would be in Lucknow by noon. "I don't know his intentions but be careful. I have been watching him and will update you if I get any info."

Kanha informed the Colonel and the team, "Devaant and his team have already reached Lucknow. If they know about Somnath temple, we must move quickly and stop them. Everyone get ready, let's move to Somnath as soon as possible. We have to first go to Lucknow and take a flight to Ahmedabad."

The Colonel said, "We can check if Devaant and his team have any flight bookings to Gujarat. You guys get ready by that time. I will go check it."

Kanha, Vivaant and Sukheshni packed their bags for the trip to Ahmedabad.

The Colonel came back worried, "Our guess was right; Devaant and his team have their flight booked for early morning, tomorrow. They will reach Ahmedabad before you guys can reach Lucknow."

Kanha said, "But they won't try anything stupid till they observe Somnath and plan. It will take at least a day for them. We will reach there by then. We can inform the local police to be extra cautious at Somnath temple. The Colonel can inform the Intelligence Bureau. We will get there by then and observe them."

The Intelligence Bureau sent a warning to the local police stating that there will be some robbery at Somnath Temple and asked them to be prepared.

The Gujarat Police guarding the Somnath temple became extra cautious and safeguarded all the temple jewelry in lockers after the pooja. They increased security to Somnath.

Devaant reached Ahmedabad at 6.30 a.m. Kanha and the team travelled overnight to reach Lucknow from the Sirkha army camp.

Devaant met some arms dealer to get a few guns and other weapons. He had ordered a Shivalinga which was a replica of Somnath, as Devaant spent the whole day in Ahmedabad and planned for the attack.

Kanha, Vivaant and Sukheshni came to Ahmedabad by evening and rested in a hotel. Kanha called Lhawang for updates.

Lhawang said that his men were trying to keep track of Devaant and the team and he were still in Ahmedabad.

Kanha was relieved after thinking to himself, "If Devaant was still at Ahmedabad, he would not have planned for an attack tonight and they had one more day to plan for it."

Kanha came and informed Vivaant and Sukheshni that Devaant still hadn't reached Somnath. They had one more day but Vivaant was looking sad.

Kanha asked Vivaant as to what was worrying him.

Vivaant asked Kanha, "Why should I fight and who am I fighting for? I have lost my father in this battle; I might lose my brother. I don't want anything.

The brother whom I should have been playing with is the one whom I am fighting against! The brother for whom my mother prays to God every single day that she will meet him one fine day is the one I am holding the gun against. I am in a big dilemma."

Kanha smiled and said, "You are sounding exactly like Arjuna on the battlefield in front of Krishna when he recited the Bhagavad-gita.

I want to mention a few things which you can relate to, Vivaant. You are not only a son to your mother but also to Mother India. You must do your karma as a son towards the nation.

The meaning of karma is to do your action and the intention behind your action is what matters.

Only the selfish and ignorant ones work towards their profit. The wise work for the welfare of the world without thinking about themselves.

Remember you are fighting to get back your brother. If you can't fight to get what you want, then you don't have the right to cry for what you lost.

Vivaant, we are mere instruments of God. Be brave, look at your dad who resisted Tarak for almost twenty years. It was his love for the nation and love for your family that gave him the strength. You must fight this battle for the love of your brother.

On this path of truth, no effort is waste, it will protect you from all your fears.

Don't think about past or future Vivaant, just live the present. Do your karma towards the truth.

You detach yourself from these feelings when you are working towards truth."

Vivaant asked, "When I have these many things going on with my life with so many attachments, how can I detach my feelings. I never understood that part of Gita. We, humans live most of our lives to please our senses. Our life gets a meaning when we act on our senses. How can we detach ourselves from our senses?"

Kanha quoted Krishna, "Detachment is not that you own nothing, detachment is that nothing owns you.

Shut out the material world and control your mind. Only then you will become free. Take your time and think about these aspects and then your mind will be clear."

Vivaant felt free from his dilemma and was now focused. He had arrived at a clear path now.

Kanha went out and contacted the Gujarat Police of Gir Somnath district and enquired about the security to Somnath temple. The police assured him that everything was under control.

Early in the morning at four O'clock Kanha, Vivaant and Sukheshni left for Gir. They stopped at a Dhaba after Rajkot near Bharudi toll plaza for breakfast on the highway.

By coincidence, Devaant's car was coming on the same highway. A hundred metres before the toll when Devaant's car slowed down at the toll queue he saw Vivaant and Sukheshni getting down and going towards the Dhaba. Devaant quickly asked his driver to take the car near the Dhaba.

Devaant ordered his boys to fix a time bomb on Vivaant's car. The driver parked his car next to Vivaant's. One guy took the time bomb silently from the trunk when no one was looking and passed it on to the other person who quickly planted it beneath the car.

Kanha, Vivaant and Sukheshni finished their breakfast and came back by which time their cab driver too returned and they started their car and proceeded towards Somnath.

Someone was trying to follow their car and were shouting something. The driver saw it but didn't care.

Kanha also observed it and saw he had five missed calls from Lhawang.

He called him back to hear a piece of news that scared him a bit saying that Devaant and his team had fixed a time bomb to a silver car.

Kanha asked the driver to stop the car and shouted at everyone to get out. As they all jumped out of the car on the road, the bomb exploded and the car was up in flames within seconds.

Vivaant ran towards Sukheshni. She was safe. They all had some injuries. Kanha walked towards them and was relieved to see everyone alive.

He said, "It seems Devaant and the team passed by and saw us. They fixed a bomb when we were having breakfast."

They reached Somnath by evening after getting first aid at Rajkot. They cleaned up and got new clothes and went to the temple.

Kanha ensured that the security was fool-proof. They had darshan of Somnath and returned to ask for permission to guard the Somnath Shivalinga.

Devaant received the news that Kanha and his team had reached, and they were paying special attention to the Shivalinga. He dropped his plan for the day to arrive at a better strategy for another day.

The next morning, Kanha and his team went to the Panch Pandava gufa to spend some time. They knew there would be no attack in the morning because of the huge crowd.

Kanha, Vivaant and Sukheshni were closely examining the caves. There were some paintings of Balarama taking the form of Adishesha and entering the cave and there was also some writing below it. Vivaant asked a guide about the writing.

The guide explained by showing the pictures and writings on the wall, "Balarama is guarding Somnath in the form of Adishesha in this cave, if any Danava tries to touch the Somnath Shivalinga, Adishesha will bring his wrath upon them."

Kanha chuckled and said, "Tarak is brilliant, that's why he has sent Devaant to fetch the Shivalinga."

Sukheshni started breathing heavily after few minutes and said, "I am feeling suffocated. I will wait outside near the water fountain, until you people see all these caves."

Vivaant and Kanha agreed and went on to see more paintings on the inner walls depicting the Pandavas staying here and some stories of the Mahabharat and when they came out near the water falls, they were unable to find Sukheshni anywhere.

They searched at all the nearby locations. She was nowhere to be found. Both of them were worried.

Kanha made a call to the local police requesting them to search. He then called Lhawang to find out if he knew anything and where Devaant and his team were staying and whether they had kidnapped her.

Lhawang said that he was trying to track them, but they were changing places quicker than expected.

Kanha said, "This must be Devaant's plan to deviate us so that he can attack tonight. We must inform the police to be careful." Vivaant was equally worried about Sukheshni and said, "We must search for her first and rescue her."

Kanha called Inspector Parth asking him to add more security at Somnath temple as the attack was probably going to happen at night and asked for help in finding Sukheshni.

Kanha got all the possible locations as to where Devaant's team might have taken her from Lhawang and began searching for her. It was difficult for them to search. They tried to track Sukheshni's cell, but it was turned off on the way to Rajkot.

At first, Kanha thought it might be a plan to distract them from Somnath and pull them to Rajkot. But they could not find Sukheshni in Somnath.

It was already late evening. If they went to Rajkot, they could not stop Devaant.

Kanha said, "Vivaant you stay here and protect the Shivalinga along with Inspector Parth. I will go and find Sukheshni and bring her. I'll take a police team and proceed to Rajkot. The police have an idea about the kidnapping and where they could have possibly taken her."

Vivaant said, "No, there is security at the temple. I can come with you."

Kanha intervened saying, "No, only you can stop your brother, so you should be present here." If there is any security alarm, Inspector Parth will be with you and take you there." Vivaant agreed and Kanha left with his team towards Rajkot.

Devaant was happy that his plan had worked out fine. Kanha had left the city and no one could stop him from getting the Shivalinga.

He asked his team to get prepared. They loaded the artificial Shivalinga on to the Jeep and left for Somnath.

At midnight under the full moon, the Somnath temple was shining as if it were made of gold. Devaant prayed God for forgiveness for the task he was about to do. His team approached Somnath carefully. All of them wore masks and black dresses.

When they neared the temple, they used drones which were in the shape of kites that hovered over the temple and gave them a clear 360-degree view about the location of all the policemen guarding Somnath.

They located all the policemen and executed their plan. They sent the next batch of drones. All guards were wondering as to how so many kites came near the temple. By that time the drones released gases which made all the police personnel unconscious.

Suddenly there was no update to the police station from the policemen guarding the Somnath temple.

A guard called from the CCTV room and said that everyone was unconscious and there was a strong odour of something and he was also feeling dizzy and he hung up.

Parth knew something was wrong. He went and picked up a few masks and took Vivaant to Somnath.

Vivaant's heart started beating faster than ever, there were lots of questions gnawing at his mind —how would he convince Vedaant? Could he convince him to surrender? What if Vedaant died here? Could he fulfil his father's last wish? Could he fulfill a mother's dreams?

As they went closer, they saw two people guarding outside. They were in a black dress wearing masks.

The police carefully surrounded the area. Vivaant and Parth went in from the rear and the police shot at the two who were at the front.

As they entered the temple, they saw two people were guarding the garbhagriha (sanctum sanctorum) as Devaant was inside trying to remove the Shivalinga with a huge magnetic field generator and another hefty guy was helping him.

Vivaant and Parth were successful in killing the two men guarding the garbhagriha by shooting at them.

Devaant and the hefty guy hid behind the doors as Parth slowly tried to get inside. The hefty guy held Parth's hand and started beating him and tried to break his arm.

Vivaant shot him in the head. Devaant quickly took his gun and aimed it at Vivaant but Parth shot his palm.

Vivaant shouted when Parth was firing at Devaant. "No, he is my brother, don't shoot him. As Parth was looking at Vivaant, Devaant hit Parth's hand with his leg and the gun fell far away from him. Vivaant shouted, "Vedaant, no, stop it!"

Devaant turned to him and asked, "Who is Vedaant?"

Vivaant said, "You are! You are the eldest son of Dr Vishwanath and my brother. Stop this nonsense and come home, a mother is waiting for you from twenty years."

"Shut up this nonsense, my father is Tarak and my name is Devaant for your information," Devaant retorted.

Vivaant smiled and said, "Oh is it, then tell me who is your mother?"

Devaant said, "I know I was adopted when I was four years old and that does not make me the son of Dr Vishwanath."

Vivaant said, "Oh! What a coincidence that you were adopted and Dr Vishwanath was kidnapped by Tarak at the same time. You were also kidnapped, my brother, not adopted. Do you even know why you are here? What is it that Tarak will do with this Shivalinga? Why did he not come here by himself?"

"He does not need to come; he has confidence in me." Devaant answered him.

"You fool, he cannot touch this Shivalinga and move it because he is a Danava, else Adishesha will rise and will finish him off," Vivaant tried to convince him.

"What nonsense are you speaking?" Devaant laughed.

"Do you even know the secret of Mt Kailash? You secured the box you should know it," said Vivaant.

Devaant fell silent

"It seems, he doesn't even want his son to know who he is and what is his goal," said Vivaant.

"This Shivalinga will open a portal to Danavaloka and will bring the Danavas here on Earth and there will be a massacre and he wants to conquer the Earth and kill millions of people and you will be responsible for it." Vivaant tried telling him the truth.

Devaant stood still for a second upon hearing this and looked at Vivaant.

"You are a good storyteller, are you hallucinating or what?" Devaant started laughing at Vivaant.

"Don't laugh like mad; if you don't want to believe me, I have the pictures of the opened box and the secrets within.

There were a lot of palm leaf scriptures in Sanskrit. If you want to look at them. Please take this." Vivaant handed over his phone to Devaant.

Devaant recognized those palm leaf scriptures and the box. He had seen them but had not got a chance to look at them. Now he read the pictures of inscriptions and was shocked. His hands were shaking and his whole world collapsed, he knew it was all built on lies.

A shocking incident passes in front of his eyes in his memory — "Was he responsible for the shooting that resulted in killing his own father?" That's why Dr Vishwanath had tears in his eyes and wanted to speak to him and he had pushed him towards the security guards. Now he remembered that horrific moment.

Devaant fell to the ground and started crying. "How can I? I killed my own father. I have no right to be on this Earth. I will die," and he tried to grab a gun and shoot himself.

Vivaant stopped him and asked him to calm down. "You didn't do it intentionally. It was all Tarak's doing. Don't think of dying, a mother is waiting to see her son from twenty years."

Parth stood up and said, "To meet your mother you must surrender yourself."

Vedaant said, "Take me, there is no punishment sufficient for what I have done. Get me the highest punishment possible."

Vivaant looked at Parth. Parth said, "I will take you under the crime of trying to steal in the Somnath temple. You should be out early."

As they came out and called Kanha they got to know he was successful in rescuing Sukheshni from the clutches of the kidnappers and was bringing her back.

They went to the police station and Kanha joined them.

Sukheshni went and hugged Vivaant and started crying. Sukheshni said, "I was so scared in life for the first time and because you were not there with me. Promise me, you will never leave me."

Vivaant smiled and said, "Yes I do, I will always be with you." Unknowingly he had become an integral part of her.

They finally went to take rest at the hotel and the next day they had darshan and enjoyed the Light Show at Somnath temple in Amitabh Bachchan's voice.

While enjoying the show, Vivaant was left with one question — When and how could he make his mother meet Vedaant and when could he complete his family as per his father's last wish."

Kanha had asked the Indian Government to put pressure on the Tibetan police to capture Tarak. But from that day onwards he was missing, he had gone underground and his companies were shut.

EPILOGUE

Six months later

Vivaant took Sukheshni on an early morning ride to Nandi Hills. It was cold and foggy. Sukheshni was enjoying the mesmerizing view while riding to the top of the hills.

They stood at the viewpoint on top near the temple enjoying the beautiful sunrise. Vivaant went and covered her eyes from behind.

All their friends surrounded her silently. Sukheshni asked, "What is it Vivaant?"

As he opened her eyes everyone shouted - "Surprise!" They had brought her a cake, and everyone started singing her the Birthday song.

She was on cloud nine. She hugged Vivaant and thanked him for this arrangement and said that this was the most beautiful birthday she had ever had.

Vivaant got a call from Kanha who asked, "Where are you Vivaant? How is Sukheshni?"

"I am doing fine Kanha, today is Sukheshni's birthday and we are celebrating at Nandi Hills. Wish her, I will hand the phone over to her." He gave the call to Sukheshni and Kanha wished her a Happy Birthday and told her to give the phone to Vivaant.

"Vivaant, I hope you are enjoying yourself; I am sorry to disturb you but I had to give you two important messages. There is a good one and a bad one. Which one would you like to hear first." Kanha asked.

"Good one!" said Vivaant.

"Your brother has got bail and he is out," said Kanha

"Oh! That's great news. I am waiting to meet him and introduce him to my mother. I want to see that smile on her face. What's the bad one?" asked Vivaant.

"There has been a burglary at Somnath temple. Your brother is missing, and he was last seen in Tarak's car with Guruji we are trying to locate them." Vivaant was shocked to hear this news from Kanha.

"I had my suspicion reverified Guruji's photo with Tarak's and they both matched. His long hairs and long beard has fooled us. Ok I will take about it later, I am busy now and will call you later," Kanha cut the call.

To be continued...

REFERENCES

This book has been made possible by the extensive research I have done to base my theories on some articles, blogs and YouTube videos. These are some of the links that I have referred to while writing the book.

1. Mass Extinctions and Periodicity by D. M. Raup and J. Sepkoski in 1984. https://www.frozenevolution. com/mass-extinctions-periodicity

2. The Great Cycles or 'YUGAS' - Isha Foundation by Sadhguru https://www.youtube.com/ watch?v=eaHVNQwO68E&t=1s

3. Videos of Ancient Aliens on History Channel https://www.youtube.com/user/historychannel

4. The four faces of Mt Kailash made of different elements are mentioned in Wikipedia referred from Allen, Charles. (1999). The Search for Shangri-La: A Journey into Tibetan History. Little, Brown and Company. Reprint: Abacus, London. 2000. ISBN 0-349-11142-1.

5. In the Puranas and the Atharvaveda, 14 lokas or worlds — seven upper and seven lower are mentioned.

6. The seven chakras & stones and their benefits are explained in the link below. https://meanings. crystalsandjewelry.com/chakras/

7. The war between Shalva and Krishna mentioned in the Bhagavat Purana is explained at the following link. https://www.booksfact.com/ technology/ancient-technology/ancient-aircraft-vimana-parachute-king-salwa-bhagavata-purana. html

8. Evidence for large anomalous nuclear explosions on Mars in the past. https://www.hou.usra.edu/meetings/lpsc2015/pdf/2660.pdf

9. Oannes and the seven seers mentioned in the Sumerian text is explained at this link. https://therealsamizdat.com/tag/seven-sages-of-sumeria/

10. The Indian Institute of Vedic Research has done ground-breaking work in arriving at the Ramayana and Mahabharata timeline. http://www.riseforindia.com/i-serve-research-on-indian-history-and-vedas/

11. The Sunken City of Dwarka https://www.youtube.com/watch?v=nQZFS9Hij0M https://www.gounesco.com/where-mythology-meets-reality-sunken-city-of-dwarka/

12. Verse and Translation of the shloka in Prologue is from Bhagavad-Gita Referred from this link. https://www.holy-bhagavad-gita.org/

13. Verse and Translation from Srimad-Bhagavatam referred from Srimad-Bhagavatam by His Divine Grace A.C. Bhaktivedanta Swami Prabhupada.

CPSIA information can be obtained
at www.ICGtesting.com
Printed in the USA
BVHW041411060723
666783BV00003B/347

9 781647 335601